"Stay with me," he said. "You have no choice."

Julian's powerful arms were around her—not with the violence that had once galvanized her into virtuoso flying leaps on stage, but with a sensuality that took her into an alien realm. While she stared up at him, half hypnotized, he lifted her boldly, then brought his mouth down on hers with a sweet savage force.

Shock waves flashed through her body, searing her veins. Even the instant of stunned resistance could not last. The scent of him was in her nostrils. She thought of wood smoke and fine leather, tangy blue air. Yet his skin was contradictory—rasping satin that pricked hers where it touched, radiating pinpoints all over her body.

Spellbound

Margaret Way

HarlequinBooks

TORONTO • NEW YORK • LOS ANGELES • LONDON
AMSTERDAM • PARIS • SYDNEY • HAMBURG
STOCKHOLM • ATHENS • TOKYO • MILAN

Original hardcover edition published in 1982
by Mills & Boon Limited

ISBN 0-373-02537-8

Harlequin Romance first edition March 1983

CHAPTER ONE

IT started for Lucie when she was seven years old and ended when she was twenty-two. Then she lay in a hospital bed wondering why the gods who had chosen to destroy her had not, in their mercy, killed her outright. Bitterness filled her and she lay there immobile, her legs that had served her faithfully shrouded in plaster, unreconciled to her fate.

Through the open door to her right, Sister Jarvis came in and with her the now familiar waft of hospital smells.

'Have you taken your medication?' The voice was gentle but bracing. 'You should, dear. You need it.'

Lucie ached to ask this good, capable woman why she needed anything. Instead she allowed yet another capsule to slide down her throat, only wishing it would bring her permanent oblivion.

'Good girl!' Sister settled her back against the pillow and gave her a little nod of encouragement. None knew better than Sister Jarvis that one could not survive and agonise over all the suffering and tragedy one saw in the course of a day, but her heart bled for this beautiful, broken little ballet dancer. Paddon-Jones had done a flawless job on that knee, but Lucienne Gerard would never dance again as she used to; to thundering cascades of applause. The broken leg would heal, the damaged bones of the foot, even the scar under the right knee would become invisible, so beautifully had the operation been performed, but she would never accomplish again what she had done in the past. Dancers of the calibre of Lucienne Gerard needed a superb physical machine; a body that would never let them down no matter what impossible demands were made upon it. Under extreme conditions it was almost certain her legs would not survive the torture that was part and parcel of virtuoso pyrotechnics.

Lucienne Gerard would be whole again, just as beautiful and infinitely graceful, but beyond that, there was nothing anyone could do. The most brilliant young principal of the spectacular new Strasberg Ballet would have to live happily ever after far away from a stage and footlights and the shouted bravos.

Sister turned away abruptly, making a sound that was intended to be heartening but came out like a little sob of shared pain. Some things hurt worse than others. A broken body to a dancer was as catastrophic as a great athlete laid low by some crippling sclerosis. It was a total loss of the body's splendid mechanism, with a separate terrible shock for the brain.

Only a month before, Sister Jarvis had seen Lucienne Gerard on stage. She had been dancing the lead role in *Black Iris*, a small masterpiece especially created for her by the remarkable Julian Strasberg. One of the finest choreographers in the world, a native of New York, he had nevertheless turned his back on one of the greatest companies in the world for the complete artistic freedom he now enjoyed as sole director of the young, emerging Strasberg Ballet, a company he had sworn to lift to the highest pinnacle of the ballet world.

Sister Jarvis, not a balletomane, regarded that even-

ing as one of the most enriching of her whole life. She
had been thrilled and enchanted—so much so that she
had been devastated when she had learned the identity
of the patient in Room 330. Why? she had asked herself. *Why?* And over and over her mind had gone back
to that wonderful night. . . .

Strasberg, a phenomenally talented man, and to
Sister's dazzled eyes staggeringly sexy, had been called
onstage afterwards to receive the audience's almost
hysterical acclaim. Lucienne Gerard, tiny beside him,
had looked surpassingly beautiful and exotic in her
black and gold costume. Against her white skin a broad
falcon collar of a queen had flashed the same gold, car-
nelian, lapis lazuli and turquoise as the gold floral circ-
let on her jet black head. Very gravely she had handed
him a single flower from her glorious bouquet; an iris,
a flower sacred to the ancient Egyptians, and the
audience had gone wild.

The ballet, a legend, had been set in the opulent
court of the Pharaoh Tuthmosis and the costumes and
the set, designed by Strasberg, had left a fairly jaded
audience, familiar with lavish sets, gasping in delight.
Already there had been a chain reaction in the fields of
fashion and interior design. They had looked splendid
together, Sister recalled romantically, almost like an
all-powerful Pharaoh and his young queen. Julian
Strasberg was a stunning man, very dark, yet not
swarthy, coal black hair and eyes, a dark golden skin.
And that mouth and those cheekbones! Just the sight
of him was enough to revitalise a woman. For all the
blazing masculinity and sheathed power, he was the
most graceful, the most pantherish man Sister Jarvis
had ever seen—or indeed expected to. He even aroused

feelings in her that she had never suspected she possessed—and just as well. As for her nurses—why, she positively had to yank them away every time he visited the ward. In reality he was a dangerous man in the sense that he had immense charisma, the capacity to fill people with strange emotions—a man from another world.

Quelling her recollections, Sister walked to the door. In the course of his career, Julian Strasberg too had suffered a permanent injury that when he was very tired left him with a slight limp. But then his talents and skills were so wide, so amazing, he did not solely rely on the life-support of a perfect machine. Lucienne Gerard, on her own admission, did. She was a dancer, an interpreter, first and last.

When she was ten, her widowed mother had denied herself every last little luxury to place Lucie in a good ballet school. Even then, her natural ability, her musicality, had been astonishing; a frail little girl with long japanned hair and enormous violet eyes. Her mother had wishes, hopes for her, and she had fulfilled them all, working tirelessly when other children were out playing; immense sacrifices made easy by her great love for her mother and her own natural genius. At fifteen she had won a scholarship to the Australian Ballet School and at sixteen, danced her first solo role with the Australian Ballet Company.

Two years later, when their cup of happiness was running over, Lucie's mother went into hospital to have an innocent little lump removed from her breast, and less than eight months later Lucie had had to be restrained at her graveside.

After that, there was no way Lucie could cope with her grief but to sublimate it in dance. When she was not dancing, she was overwhelmed. The only way she could keep herself together, to bear her lonely life, was to dance. It was what her mother had sacrificed her life for—so that Lucie, one day, could be a famous ballerina. It had been more than a dream, Lucie's mother had *believed* it. So Lucie lived with her heartbreak, imagining her mother could still see her . . . lightning-fast turns, perfect balances, penchés, dazzling fouettés, grands jetés that hung in the air . . . often with the tears coursing down her face.

In a small but radiant little role, Julian Strasberg had first seen her. At that time he had been touring with the World Ballet and while there formulated his own plans. His was from a distinguished background; a father famous as an architect, a mother equally famous as one of the four greatest ballerinas of her time. Of mixed parentage, German and Russian, Julian Strasberg had been taken to the United States as a child. There, his mother and father realised brilliant careers, but the young Julian was a rebel, an enfant terrible. Though his father had insisted he train as an architect, for all his inherited ability, the world of theatre and dance came to occupy the most important place in his heart and his brain. He could have been a great dancer himself had he devoted himself to that medium, but it seemed he only wanted to know how dancers' bodies worked.

What he really wanted, his mother was once quoted as saying, was to create a whole new ballet repertoire; one that made tremendous demands on the company. His *own* company, so he could enjoy absolute control. Julian Strasberg, for all his enormous brilliance, was well known to be a raging tyrant.

In time, the tremendously gifted Camilla Price, an international star and undoubtedly an ex-lover, joined him. So too did several others, but still he set about seducing the youthful Lucienne Gerard to his side. A flawless technician as his mother once had been, she was, as he often told her, in class and in private, deeply repressed. She needed to suffer, and the minute she was part of his Company he dedicated himself to that task, sometimes reacting violently, turning the full force of his anger on her, when the others would have been ecstatic had they been able to dance like Lucienne. Her agility was perfection, yet he continued to make inhuman demands on an already exceptional technique. As for her feelings, it was obvious to everyone, he did not consider she had any. She simply existed to be punished. Yet it was evident that he had planned *Black Iris* around her right from the beginning. Julian Strasberg was a monster and Lucienne Gerard was his prize victim.

In nightmares, the minutes before the car crashed came back to Lucie in shocking detail. Joel, angry and jealous and in his jealousy sounding ugly. . . .

'Damn it, he's unspeakably cruel to you, then you let him *kiss* you!'

'I don't remember.' She truly didn't. They had been rehearsing all evening and now she was so tired the tears were streaming down her cheeks.

'I wish I could believe it.' Joel was livid with a blinding sex jealousy. 'Does it turn you on, being humiliated and bullied? He never takes his eyes off you. Picking on you when you're perfect. You can handle every dance step in creation, yet he's determined to crush you beneath his feet. And what do *you* do? You act the little coward—taking it, forever taking it when the rest of us would be screaming uncontrollably. And then, the one minute he's gentle with you, you just melt into his arms!'

'To keep from falling,' she had protested hopelessly. Julian Strasberg had arms like steel. He could lift her—he *did* lift her, showing Joel and Damien how to make her soar or how to catch her a bare inch from the floor. No one held her like he did.

Joel was not even listening, he was so full of hating. 'I think under it all, he wants you. Him and his love affairs! Just imagine Camilla Price giving up A.B.T. to chase Strasberg half way across the world!'

'Other stars did the same.' Lucie had found herself defending her tormentor. 'He's an extraordinary man—a revolutionary, almost certainly a great man. Working with a well established company wasn't what he wanted. . . .'

'Oh, no,' Joel had turned to jeer at her. 'He wanted something new, far away, so he could dominate everybody. There's such a thing as having too much creative energy, don't you know? You don't really think we're going to hold him in this country for long. So much for building up a world company! He just wants time to try out his ideas. Somewhere new in case he fails or maims one of his dancers. He wants *you*—whether to create things around you or to destroy you I don't know. There's some terrible relationship between you, and don't think Camilla doesn't know. She's ready to attack you with her nails.'

'Please stop, Joel!' she had begged him, disturbed by so much anger and violence. Everything was so different, and she was totally unprepared for it.

'But I *love* you!' he had shouted. 'Doesn't it mean something? Or do you prefer savages like Strasberg?'

Lucie had been horribly unnerved. Her eyes shut fast to stop the rush of exhausted tears, she too missed the lorry coming fast around the bend in the road. Joel saw it too late. He swerved instinctively and braked, but the car slithered out of control. It slewed hard into a guard rail and came to a crushing, grinding halt. The passenger side had borne the brunt of the crash. Joel sustained a minor head injury on the moment of impact, otherwise he miraculously escaped.

Lucie had not seen him since.

There were always flowers in her room and for the first two weeks a constant stream of visitors, people from her own world, and after a while they all came to see it as a cruelty. How could anyone speak brightly of Lucie's future? They had all heard she was finished as a dancer. It was not even possible to speak about personalities or performances—dear God, not to a girl whose life's dream was gone. In the end it seemed like a kindness to leave her alone. Only Julian Strasberg continued to come, for heaven knows what reason. Julian Strasberg and Joel's mother.

That afternoon, when she was at her lowest, Joel's mother called again.

'Won't you see her?' Sister begged sadly.

'No.' Lucie turned her head away, so much beauty and poignancy in the little movement that Sister's throat tightened.

'But she's in anguish, Lucie.' She had come to call the girl by her name, acutely aware her compassion was bordering on distress for herself. 'She told me she hasn't heard one word from her son since he disappeared.'

'I'm sorry,' Lucie said automatically, in a low voice. 'But what can *I* do?' She did not even glance down at her legs. 'Joel wrecked my life. I expect he'll wreck his mother's. There's nothing either of us can do about it. It's our destiny, our unhappy fate.'

'But there *is* something you can do for her,' Sister Jarvis persisted, as much for Lucie as for the lost, bewildered woman who was seated down the corridor. 'You'll come out of this, Lucie, I know you will. You don't ask, but you're making rapid progress. You're a very strong little person really, for all your apparent fragility. Very strong and disciplined through your dancing. You know how to live with pain and terrible disappointments. Mrs Tennant has no such strength. She's in despair and terribly worried about her son. You can help her, even from a hospital bed.'

Lucie was silent, but she turned her head back and looked up into Sister's grave face. 'She never wanted to meet me before,' she said.

Sister was flabbergasted, her eyes roving over the girl's exquisitely refined features. 'But I thought. . . .'

'Yes?' The huge violet eyes were quite without bitterness.

'That you two were engaged—or about to be.'

'No.' Lucie clasped her small, slender hands together. 'I made no commitment to Joel. All I've had all my life was my dear mother and my career.'

'But his mother thinks you were very much in love!'

Sister blurted out, indicating her shock.

The porcelain-skinned face went even tighter and more intense. 'Joel was my friend, a dear friend and a good partner. And I was wrong to think that.'

'Oh, Lucie!' The whole tragedy was striking Sister too forcibly these days. She could not rid her mind of that wonderful evening when Lucienne Gerard, ballerina, had been whole and triumphant. 'You won't see her?'

'No.' For a mere instant the violet eyes were awash with tears. 'I'm not angry with Joel. I expect in his own way he's as devastated as I am. I don't want him to punish himself or his mother. I'm sorry for both of them, but I don't want to see either of them. Ever.'

Sister responded quietly, restoring some measure of tranquillity. 'All right, my dear. Mrs Tennant has a family. They will have to solve the problem of Joel.'

Lucie was asleep when Julian Strasberg arrived, and he instantly perceived that her dream was troubled. He stood over her, watching her attentively and as a shudder racked her body he said firmly, '*Lucienne*.'

'No,' she muttered, still in the grip of torment.

'Wake up!'

Her eyes flew open, as though she instantly recognised the tone.

'Ah, yes, you've been dreaming. Bad dreams.'

'About you.' It was a tremendous effort for her to speak to him, but she knew she had to because he would not go away.

'So what was I doing, little one?' He eased himself into a chair, a faint smile on his striking, hateful face.

'You wanted me to hold a penché until every bone in my body was screaming to relax.'

'And did you?'

'Perhaps. What does it matter?'

'You look better.' He ignored the constant signs of anguish, the terror that was in her.

'I believe Sister said the same thing.'

'An excellent woman.' There was a hint of amusement in his voice. 'You know, in another week you'll be ready to go home.'

'How lovely.' She gave him a brilliant glance. The very air around him crackled with vibrant charges and there was absolutely no pity in those heathenish eyes. 'Is that what the doctors say?'

'I speak to them regularly.'

'I know.' The terrible uncertainty in her quickened. 'What I don't know is *why*?'

'If you could, you'd run from me. Hide for shelter.'

'You've seen my legs.' She felt as though he had struck her a terrible blow.

'The plaster will come off. Two months at the outside. Everything that could be done *has* been done for you. The worst will pass.'

'I know.' She laughed helplessly. 'The truth is I would never have found the dedication to stay with you. All that sweat and punishment—it was too much. It will be wonderful to be away from ballet.'

'One side of it, perhaps,' he said deliberately. 'But it is your life and your world.'

Her lovely face registered her shock and confusion. '*No-no-*' she stammered. 'You know very well I can never go back.'

'Why not?' He pulled his chair closer and took her

hand so she was required to look at him.

'You're cruel, aren't you?' she shuddered. 'It takes a cruel person to ask that.'

'So I broke my ankle.' The striking, ruthless face was appraising her critically.

'You told me it was a skiing accident.'

'Just so, but the injury remained.'

'For God's sake!' She tried to pull away from him, but it was impossible. 'You never really wanted to be a dancer.'

'I don't know that I *wanted* a broken ankle. It happened, and only persistent effort has made me as mobile as I am.' Lucie had turned her face away and he caught her chin. 'I insist you listen to me.'

The lean strong fingers were hurting her. 'If you only knew how I hate you!'

'God, no, darling,' he said witheringly, 'take my word for it, as far as emotions are concerned, you're just a little baby.'

'At least to you.' He was still holding her, vicelike, and it was curious how his vitality and strength was reaching to the centre of her being. She realised she wanted to hit him, for the first time fighting the domination of body and mind.

'Poor little Lucie!' he breathed the words mockingly.

She did not know how long she lay there staring into his eyes. From time to time she had registered his beauty and his maleness, now she found herself studying him closely; not as a prowling panther who took delight in drilling her to exhaustion but as a man, the veteran of countless affairs, including Camilla, the ballerina he had brought into his Company.

'Tell me what you see,' he said lightly, his long eyes narrowing.

'A monster.'

'You aren't serious?'

'A suberb monster, but a monster nevertheless.' Her huge violet eyes swept over his face, thinking it extraordinary. Power and ruthlessness were tangible, a matching sensuality. A voluptuous woman like Camilla would revel in such virility, but Lucie found it frightening and overpowering. She, who had never had a lover in a world where love was a game.

His had a very definite, very foreign face clearly showing his ancestry. Thick, springing jet black hair, wide brow, very pronounced cheekbones, deep-set, almond-shaped, brilliant black eyes, hawkish, high-bridged nose, generous mouth, disturbing mouth, the edges very cleanly cut, squarish, deeply cleft chin. His teeth, like the American he had become, were white and perfect, flashing against his dark golden skin every time he smiled. His smile was totally disarming, especially after his snarl.

Even without the intensifying factor of his mind, his looks would have been extraordinary, but everything he was, the brilliance, the hot temper, the uncommon, burning energy, was so clearly apparent in that compelling face. Lucie hardly dared to keep looking at him, unquestionably troubled by the excitement he engendered. Except for the great love she had borne for her mother, her heart had known utmost quiet.

'Don't spare my feelings,' he said, with a twist of his mobile mouth.

'You never tried to spare mine.'

'What did you expect? I would scream at a nothing?'

She shook her head. 'Joel was terribly jealous of you,' she whispered.

'Let it out,' he said harshly.

'I don't think I can.'

'It will be better.'

Lucie lay back and gave a faint moan. 'His mother keeps trying to see me.'

'I know. Tell me about Joel.'

She shut her eyes and her lashes lay very black and heavy against a camellia-white skin. 'We were arguing. Joel was arguing. He was angry. He said you were cruel to me and I didn't have to take it.'

'He said he wanted you.'

'He said he loved me.'

'Where *is* he?' This very flatly in a voice that could purr like black velvet.

'I don't know—should I?' She opened her lovely eyes again and stared at the ceiling. 'I suppose he's blaming himself dreadfully.'

'That's exactly what he should do,' Julian said sternly.

'You sound angry.' She turned her head and met his eyes and what she saw in them made her catch her breath. 'It was an *accident*!' she insisted.

'So.' Now his expression was masked. 'I'm not a kind person.'

'No, not kind at all.' She gave a queer little laugh. 'What's to become of me?'

'You come to me.' He said it matter-of-factly as though it was the most ordinary thing in the world.

'*You?*'

'Why are you looking at me so oddly? You have no one else to look after you, and you'll need looking after until you're out of plaster.'

Was it possible she *could* get out of hospital? That someone was really offering to look after her? Though she was conscious of a rise in spirits she still said, 'But I can't stay with you. That's absolutely out of the question.'

'Is it? I have a nice house, plenty of room. Terraces where you can sun yourself—your legs, not your face.'

Lucie found that her hands were trembling uncontrollably. 'But it's not suitable. People will talk.'

'There will be nothing for them to talk about,' he said with his customary arrogance. 'I know you've been fretting about having to remain in hospital.'

'Yes.' Her hair had come out of its soft chignon, now it floated down her back in a stream of raven silk. The pain and terror of the past weeks had curiously not drained, but enhanced her beauty. She looked like a figurine in priceless porcelain, graceful and delicate, demanding the gentlest handling. Even the enveloping blue nightgown she was wearing could not hide the exquisite contours of her upper body or the reality of her singular grace.

Now she stared at him out of her flower-bright eyes. 'Please tell me what I must really do?'

'I am telling you.' Her agitation did not affect him at all. He was completely composed. 'There's nothing to be frightened of. You need security and I'm going to provide it. Think of it only as a way out of your predicament.'

'I could ask one of the girls to stay with me.'

'Absurd. You need a man to lift you—a male nurse.'

She shook her head hopelessly. 'I'll have to stay here.'

'No, little one.' He spoke with faint exasperation. 'You're going to do as you're told. I am your Director. When your legs are out of plaster, you may go back to your own little abode.'

'And you're going to discuss this with Camilla?' She realised the moment she said it she had made a mistake.

'Now why should I do that?' Julian spoke in his softest voice, a voice to make one shiver.

'I thought. . . .' Her heavy eyelashes flickered.

'Yes?' he asked with cold disdain.

'People will talk.' All that endless delicious gossip.

'Shall I marry you, then, darling?' he offered acidly. 'For how many weeks it takes for you to get on your feet.'

'Maybe I'm not as worldly as you.' Her beautiful eyes filled with tears. She was completely unsure of his motive for suggesting this; troubled by its implications.

'It's all settled,' he said curtly, his flaring black brows drawing together. 'You are a child in need of shelter. Your injuries preclude any other speculation. You are so exceedingly helpless you must either remain here and become increasingly introspective or be taken into somebody's care. I feel I have a responsibility to a leading member of my company. People can think what they like—they do in any case. My conduct, I assure you, will be fatherly.'

Despite herself she laughed. Her first real laugh since the accident.

'Well, brotherly,' he smiled, and his almond eyes crinkled at the corners. From intimidating to flashing charm.

'I'll think about it,' she said. Hospital was an alien place, a place to be away from, yet she was aware of all the relative crises in staying with him.

'Of course.' He stood up in one incredibly lithe movement. 'Think about it by all means, but it's exactly what will happen.'

CHAPTER TWO

ON the day Lucie was due to go home, Camilla Price made her ominous first and last visit. She swept into Lucie's room and the face of the nurse who was attending Lucie lit up in entranced recognition. Camilla Price was a stunningly attractive woman, not a beauty, but looking, acting and standing as if she were.

'Miss Price!' The little nurse fell back from the bed, as most people fell back for Camilla.

'How are you?' Camilla gave her a brilliant, empty smile.

It was apparent Camilla required no answer, nor indeed would have heard it had one been supplied, so the young nurse excused herself and hurried from the room. So *that* was the great Camilla Price, heavily made up and wearing the most gorgeous clothes. In an odd way she was an extremely handsome woman, but not, the little nurse thought shrewdly, very kind.

As soon as the nurse had gone, Camilla came directly to the point.

'You are *not* to go with Julian!' The expression on her face was appallingly vehement.

'I don't want to, you know.' Lucie went white at her aggression.

'Then why is this?'

'I have no alternative,' Lucie said with a terrible

depression. Sister had not appeared to help her dress, so she was still lying in the hospital bed.

'Can't you get a nurse?' Camilla demanded. 'Surely you can pay someone to look after you?'

'I'll be lucky if I have anything left after I pay the hospital. And there's still my operation to be paid for.'

'Am I right in thinking you're going to persist with this?' Camilla came closer, her strange yellowish-brown eyes glaring.

'I'm sorry, Camilla,' said Lucie. 'There are very few courses open to me. I don't think you know what it's like to be physically helpless.'

'I don't think *you* know what it's like to cross me!'

'I don't see how I could do that,' Lucie said in a strangled whisper. She was the very opposite of a violent person and Camilla's ugly animosity left her dazed.

'Be careful,' Camilla warned her, 'and take that innocent look off your face. Oh, you think you're so clever, persuading Julian to take you in. How sad for you that I found out in time. Did you *really* think your little tragedy would bring you together? Julian despises you as a woman; a shut-in little virgin born to be bullied. His interest in you was as a dancer, and you are no longer that.'

'No.' Inside Lucie was sick and trembling, but her voice was quiet. 'Why do you hate me, Camilla? I'm no threat to you in any way.'

'Certainly not.' The yellow eyes glowed malignantly. 'Anyway, I'm not going to have you getting in my way. You can't possibly stay with Julian. He's a famous man. *I* am famous. People will talk.'

'I've *said* this to him!' Lucie's violet eyes looked

positively haunted. 'You should know he doesn't listen to anyone.'

'That's not true of me!' Camilla was controlling herself with difficulty. 'I'm a person of importance in Julian's life. I want to tell you this. We're lovers, bound to one another. You can't begin to grasp what we mean to each other. We may not marry, but what does that mean? In our world, nothing. I will not *permit* you to stay in his house.'

'Very well,' Lucie answered her in a lifeless tone.

'You mean that?' Camilla actually fell back, falling into a naturally dramatic pose.

'I'm quite aware that you're Julian Strasberg's mistress. It means nothing to me, just as *he* means nothing except as a brilliant man. A sorcerer, I suppose, who holds us all spellbound.'

Camilla came forward and struck the chair with violence. 'He means nothing, yet you call him a sorcerer? For that's exactly what he is. He has power, Julian. Too much power for his own good. People recognise it at once. My God, hasn't he transformed *my* life!'

'Find him and tell him not to come.'

Camilla gave a rather sinister laugh. 'Tell him yourself. Tell him you've made other plans. That crazy boy, Joel—go to him. Stay with his mother. I hear she's been haunting the ward.'

'At least she had the sensitivity not to come in,' retorted Lucie.

'Touché!' Camilla laughed again. 'I have no sensitivity, my dear, only on stage. Julian doesn't really care about you at all. He can see you're stupidly frightened—even *I* can see that. I suppose if the worst comes to the worst I can lend you money until you find work. How much would you want?'

This is all unreal! Lucie thought. If only I could *walk*! She saw then her dancing as something of the past; another girl, another life, full of wonderful aspirations. Sunlight caught the sheen of her hair, making it look as though it was strung with sequins.

'Well?' Camilla prompted, only wishing to see the end of this remarkable girl. 'I have to dance tonight. I think you could let me have your answer.'

There was nothing left to Lucie but pride. 'I'll manage, Camilla, somehow.'

Camilla's golden eyes had the brilliant, predatory look of a hunting hawk. 'And you'll tell Julian?'

'If he'll listen.'

'*Make* him listen.' Camilla came even closer and Lucie caught the wave of her powerful, musky scent. 'If you're to have any peace at all, don't attempt to cross me. You're not equal to it.'

The evidence of this struck Lucie forcibly. She could feel the vibrations from the older woman's body, the dangerous hostility. Camilla had hated her from the very first day she had joined the Company, sensing a rival even as Julian Strasberg tore her technique and interpretation to shreds.

Afterwards when Sister came Lucie told her there had been a change of plan. Julian Strasberg would be unavoidably delayed at the theatre, so she was to travel by ambulance to her own little flat and there he would collect her some time after the evening's performance.

Sister, who for some reason had found Julian Strasberg's attendance on her favourite patient very romantic, fell for it at once.

'The ambulance men will look after you, my dear.' She smiled down at Lucie, imprisoned in a wheelchair. 'Now you know when you're to come back to have the plaster off and after that, we'll talk about therapy.' Unexpectedly she swooped down and kissed Lucie's pale cheek. 'God bless, and chin up. You're only going to be in that wheelchair for a few more weeks. Some people are helpless all their lives.'

'I know.' Lucie gave her a resigned look from her large violet eyes. 'Thank you for everything you've done for me. I know some days were difficult.'

'No.' Sister shook her steel-grey, ordered head. 'I don't think you actually realise how brave you really are.'

In the ambulance Lucie felt no necessity to keep that stiff upper lip. She was sick with nerves and agitation wondering at Julian Strasberg's reaction. She had not even left a message telling him to stay away. He would come to the hospital expecting to find her; instead he would find an empty bed.

'Are you sure you're going to be all right, love?' Tom, the younger of the two ambulance men, looked at her anxiously. They had her seated on the old velvet sofa and she looked very tiny and wan.

'Yes, of course. It won't be long.' She was grateful her mother had never had to witness her tragedy.

'When is your friend coming?' the older man asked, opening out the windows.

'Very soon.' Lucie could not have been more frightened. However hard she tried to quiet her jangled nerves she had had too much experience of Julian Strasberg's temper and habit of command. He would be furious with the loss of his precious time, more furious at her daring to alter his decision.

'What about a cup of tea before we go?' There was fascination in Tom's face as well as professional kindness.

'No, thank you—really, I'll be fine.' Lucie looked up to smile at him, a poignant illumination that washed over her exquisite little face. All the time he was reminded of a broken bird he had once found in his garden and nursed back to flight.

They stayed for a few minutes more, checking the flat, then with an encouraging word they were gone. As long as the young lady had someone to look after her, they had to get on with the job. Lucie looked at his watch. It was quarter past two.

For the next two hours Lucie's tension mounted. Any moment she expected to hear a car pull up at the front of her block of flats, then a moment later to hear a violent knocking at her door. She was almost hysterical wondering how she was going to cope with his anger, but then in the middle of it, she went to sleep, worn out with anxieties and the terrible weight of her legs. He had paid the hospital bill. He had not been meant to, but he had paid without a word. She could not even reflect on his reasons; his complex plans to rescue her from her misery. He was not a kind man. Who should know better than she?

When she opened her eyes again, he was sitting opposite her, quietly unnerving, as though he had a perfect right to be there.

'Oh——'

'Hello, Lucie.'

She was uncertain of his mood. The brilliant eyes seemed calm. He looked neither angry nor surprised.

'I'm sorry. Did you come looking for me?' It was a

stupid question, but he did not answer in his usual acid fashion.

'Sister told me your little tale.'

'You have a right to be angry.' How intolerable it was to be pinned to a sofa, to have to lie back against the cushions when she wanted to flee.

'You've acted incredibly foolishly,' he told her. 'Why?'

'I can't live in your house.' Her eyes glittered and suddenly her cheeks were hot.

'You mean you think I might try to seduce you?'

'It wouldn't be easy,' she said dryly, thereby surprising herself.

'That plaster will only be on for a short time.'

Something in his tone made her stare at him. In a black polo-necked sweater and black cords, he looked more than ever the lean, muscular, big cat. His shoulders were wide, so too the strong rib cage, but he was lean-waisted, narrow-hipped over long legs. He was beautiful, and he was just sitting there playing some sort of a subtle cat-and-mouse game.

'It would be too . . . intimate,' Lucie dragged out. 'I don't know you. You don't know me.'

He laughed aloud, mocking her and her reasoning. 'What is there to know about you, little one? Up until now your whole life has been your mother and your dancing. You've never lived. You've certainly never loved a man. This is understandable—both you and your mother preferred not to let anything get in the way of your career.'

'So?' For the first time since he had known her Lucie's darkly hyacinthine eyes flashed fire. 'My mother did without *everything* so I could get to be a good dancer!'

'Then it still remains for you to do so.'

His cruelty was so awful her revulsion showed in her face. 'You know I'll never dance again.'

'That has not been made so clear to me.' he said decisively.

'What do you mean?' She was terrified of hoping.

'I mean,' he held her eyes deliberately, 'Paddon-Jones knows a great deal, but he doesn't know dancers. Kamenova had two operations done on her kneecap. She suffered great pain, but no one attempted to stop her from trying to continue her career. Even her doctors. The human machine is very very complex and possibly more under the control of the mind than we think. Kamenova regained her excellent technique. But then she had courage to an extreme degree. She was a great dancer, not merely a talented little girl.'

'Talented,' she said bitterly. 'For *me*, great praise.'

'So why should you long for me to praise you?' He stood up and came over to her in one fluid movement.

In spite of herself Lucie made her body small so that he could sit down sideways on the sofa beside her. There was something altogether different about him tonight and she did not know what it was. 'I can't allow you to raise my hopes,' she said quietly, in a voice that would have brought a pang to anyone else but Julian Strasberg's throat. 'My career as a dancer is over. I know it. You know it. The whole ballet world knows it now. Not everyone thought me so ungifted as you. I was offered a place ... oh, no matter. I'm nothing now.' She turned her face away from him in despair.

'You're beautiful,' he said as he might have offered stupid or conceited or ugly.

'What use is *that*?' Better to be plain and have the full use of unblemished legs.

'Well, it's something,' he said dryly. 'Look at me, Lucie.' His hand was on her face now, sliding beneath her chin.

Shivers were zigzagging along her spine, unfamiliar sensations that troubled her. 'What a calamitous day!' her feelings escaped in a deep sigh.

'Sister told me you had a visitor,' he said.

She was reluctant to meet his eyes, but she had to, for those strong fingers were lightly forcing. 'I've had lots of visitors.' Why, oh, why did she have to deal with him? He was so ruthless and so strong.

'Not, I think, Camilla. That must have been her first time?'

'Yes.' She pushed her head back against the cushions and he let her go.

'And she told you you must fend for yourself?'

'She's right,' Lucie said briefly.

'Even though you can't even lock your door.' His eyes sparkled like black diamonds.

'Wasn't it locked?' She bit her lip.

'No,' he said moodily. 'Anyone could have looked through that glass panel and seen you. You fold up most beautifully, and there's that rug across your legs. They could have tried the door, as I did. You don't read the newspapers?'

'I can always lock it in future. It was an oversight.'

'It's not possible for you to stay alone,' he told her.

'And you don't have the power to dictate to me,' Lucie retorted. 'Not any longer.'

'You want a little mutiny?' It was obviously said to annoy her.

'I want you to leave me alone. Not to associate yourself with me.'

'Even as your gaoler?' He took hold of her cold hands and panic started in her mind.

'Why are you doing this?' she begged him.

'I do so many things,' he shrugged his wide shoulders.

'I'm going to give you the money for my hospital bill.'

'You can do when you come back to the Company.'

'You're a *fiend*, aren't you?' she said bitterly.

'Absolutely.' Though she resisted as much as she was able, he still held her hands, warm now from contact with his own. 'You'll be able to work for me in some capacity. Your world is ballet. If we see you can no longer really dance then we shall find something else.'

'I don't *want* anything else!' she hurled at him, sitting forward so urgently that their faces were only inches apart. 'I'm a dancer—I *was* a dancer. I can't do anything else. I couldn't even do *that*, according to you.'

'So why did I make a ballet around you?' he enquired silkily, not even reacting to her violent tone.

'I can't think why.' She looked desperate and defiant. 'You made Camilla my enemy.'

'There are always enemies in the ballet world—those who are jealous because you're a good deal better.'

'Better than Camilla?' She looked up at him with implacable disbelief.

'All right, so I threw you to the lions! The ballet was a triumph. I've had cables from all over the world. Everyone has heard; now they want to see.'

'They'll never see *me*,' Lucie said bitterly.

'Don't sound so sorry for yourself. At your best I doubt you have everything to make a ballerina. Three or four I can think of, but not you.'

'I'd almost forgotten what you're like—tearing me to bits!'

'It helped you a lot,' he pointed out.

The truth of that kept her silent, and the silence lengthened. Incredibly Julian still held her hands, and she remembered too that he had held them when they wheeled her back to her room after the operation. She had been barely conscious of anything then, but she remembered the warmth and strength of those hands. He was such a dominant person—too dominant at times, and she was bewildered by the extent of his grasp on her life. It seemed he wanted her pinned beneath his paw, but now that she was finished as a dancer, it puzzled her greatly why. Even now he should be at the theatre, within the orbit of his dancers: Camilla, his prima ballerina, down to the least significant member of the corps.

'Shouldn't you be gone from here?' she asked distractedly. 'Camilla told me she would be dancing.'

'Camilla can manage without me.'

'You should go at once.' She touched his wrist and glanced at his gold watch.

'You little fool.' He held up her chin with his hand. 'How did you think you were going to manage? Trapped on a sofa, unable to move, left to starve?'

Her violet eyes implored his understanding. 'I was going to ring Joel's mother.' The telephone was right by her hand.

'*What?*' His expression was daunting, even faintly shocked.

'What on earth *could* I do?' She started to cry. 'I'd got myself out of hospital. I couldn't come to you. I have no one, do you understand? No one. No refuge.'

'And in your terrible straits you preferred Joel's mother to *me*?' Had she not been so broken it was obvious he would have shaken her.

'There are only two things in Camilla's life—her dancing and you!'

'Stop crying.' His eyes met hers with the familiar hardness of command.

'I'm sorry.' Lucie brushed her face with her hand impatiently.

'Camilla is nothing to me.' His black head was thrown back and his brilliant eyes half closed.

'Don't take me for a complete fool!'

'But I do.' His faintly foreign accent, European, not American, was exaggerated.

'Well, that's fine, but in this particular instance, we all know about you and Camilla.'

'It sounds scorching.' He was a past master at registering disdain.

'I realise it's none of my business.' She had to lean back against the red and gold cushions.

'My God, no!' he agreed.

'Camilla is very much against my coming to stay with you.'

'All right. So what else is the problem?' He stood up impatiently and Lucie had the giddy feeling he was going to tower over her for ever.

'You don't think it *is* one?' she parried.

'I can't answer to every woman I've made love to. Besides, Camilla was years ago.'

'She still feels things very deeply.' Whether what he said was true or not, she could scarcely argue it out with him.

'Women can be very disagreeable.' He leaned back

against a cabinet and closed his eyes. 'That's why I'm not married.'

'I hope you never change your mind.'

The little waspish comment, so completely out of character, made him laugh. 'But how amusing!' Mockery pulled at his long, sensuous mouth. 'What's happened to my timid little Lucienne?'

'Tragedy.' She removed the fleecy rug with some force. 'What else could make me dream of crossing swords with the great Julian Strasberg? You've been a devil in my mind.'

'I am still,' he informed her, 'but for a short time, I can be kind.' He turned about and picked up a golden suede jacket, thrusting into it with innate grace. 'Don't reflect too much on what Camilla had to say. Anyone who disturbs you has to answer to me.'

'Are you going?' Her treacherous helplessness made her voice tremble.

'For a very short time,' he answered in a quiet, matter-of-fact tone. 'To overcome all your little embarrassments I've engaged an excellent nurse for you. She's possibly the biggest woman I've ever seen, but Sister Jarvis assured me every inch is solid gold. It wouldn't worry me to look after you myself, but of course it would worry you. Then again, Nurse Chandler is our chaperone.'

'You seem to have thought of everything.' She was filled with enormous relief.

'Of course.' He bowed mockingly, magic in his every little move. 'I'm going to fetch her now. Beside her, you'll look like a tiny child.'

From the very first moment Jessie Chandler laid eyes

on the stricken and vulnerable Lucie, she was devoted to her, and she was a first-rate nurse. Six feet and a little bit in her stockings, Jessie was a heavily built, vigorous woman, without being in the least fat. It was all big bones and solid muscle, and underneath the first astonishment, Lucie came to depend on her utterly and really care.

Jessie was extremely strong, extremely patient, and emphatically kind. Every little thing that had become tinged with embarrassment and worry in Lucie's sensitive mind, Jessie sailed over heroically, making Lucie chuckle endlessly when she had been expecting severe depression.

'Dear Jessie!' she often found herself giggling, aware that had she been left in hospital, isolated and greatly indolent, she might later have needed psychiatry. No matter the utterly ludicrous situations that seemed to arise, Jessie handled it all with gentle, humorous and downright motherly tact.

Julian liked her too, and as there was nothing much wrong with Jessie, the appreciation was mutual. As Jessie told Lucie roguishly, she had never met a man outside fiction who could make her believe in 'volcanic desires'. A while later Lucie had found herself staring at Julian until he had turned around and asked her if she was feeling feverish.

'Do you wonder?' Jessie had looked at her and winked.

The whole atmosphere while Lucie was waiting for the plaster to come off was extraordinary. Though it had seemed hardly likely to Lucie that she would ever smile again, Julian and Jessie between them attracted her to all kinds of pursuits and discussions, so she had little spare time to suffer. The house was always full of music and though she had groaned in agony when the first of the ballet suites started, Julian had cried at her to listen.

'Listen, listen,' he had said. 'Listen whenever possible. Some I know don't hear the music at all, just jump up and down.'

'How about that?' Jessie was always there to look towards her and chuckle.

In the evenings when Julian came home he brought flowers and wine and lots of things that were party-like and all three of them sat down and became mildly drunk. At least Lucie did. The other two seemed able to dispose of alcohol a whole lot better. Then when it was time for bed, Julian would scoop Lucie up while Jessie told them she was trying at all costs to break her own leg. Not once did either woman hear the bite of the infamous Strasberg tongue, but Lucie knew in her fragile bones it could not last. Hadn't he promised her a short period of kindness? She was being treated like a pet kitten, but behind all the easy charm and solicitude she knew he was the same Strasberg.

As for the rest, the house was beautiful, the view of the harbour magnificent, and Julian had obviously made it clear there were to be no visitors. Even so, Lucie steeled herself and indeed warned Jessie they could have a surprise visit from Camilla Price.

'I suppose he finds it a nuisance being so damned attractive to women!' Jessie mused. 'If she gets in, count on me.'

Though they both waited, Camilla never found her way through the subtropical grounds and life went on. She knew she was being cherished, that two very different people were being wonderfully supportive, but reality would return with the removal of the casts.

On the morning that was to happen, Lucie was sick with nerves.

'I feel terrible,' she confided to Jessie.

Jessie nodded. 'Just remember you had the best there is. Take it from an old admirer of Freddie Jones—never Paddon-Jones in the old days—so stop worrying, lass.'

It was easier said than done. You worked at being brave, at accepting the end of a promising career, but underneath like a turbulent subterranean stream was the agony at the loss of power. Was life just a series of terrible tricks? She had never hurt anyone in her life. She had worked so hard. Well, that was how it was. It had happened to others, so much worse, things that were fatal. The start of the day and she was desperately weary. Even the wine Julian had given her had not put her to sleep. The last few weeks had been a curious limbo. She had been handled so carefully she had felt almost consoled. Now came the real test, accepting her enforced fate.

'Lucie——' Julian crossed the room to look at her, his fingers touched her pale cheeks.

'I'm afraid.' She looked it, her eyes swamping her face.

'Don't see it like that,' he spoke almost harshly. 'It's more like a special day. The casts will come off and you can begin therapy.'

'Yes,' she said, looking even more terrible and too slight to sustain another moment's grief. I'll never be whole any more, she thought. Never a dancer.

Shortly after the ambulance arrived and to Lucie's

surprise Julian and not Jessie made to come with her. Jessie smoothed her brow and looked down into the lovely, clouded eyes. 'Everything will be all right, love. Julian is with you and I'll be waiting when you get home.'

Home! She did not have a home any longer. The unexpected, the extraordinary was over. In the ride to the hospital she lived through the past weeks all over again. It was a dream. Of course it was a dream, part terrible, part beautiful, out of pity. Even Julian had become affected.

'You're not going to break, are you?' he asked tersely.

'What?' she flushed with shock, lost in her tearless, depressed state.

'Let's forget about your legs. What about your plans?'

'I don't know. I don't know.'

His expression darkened. 'Well, my advice is, stay in there. It's been terrible, but that's life. Just don't go retiring yourself.'

His firmness after so much indulgence left her dazed. 'You didn't *have* to come with me,' she said in a strangled whisper.

'You don't want me here?'

'Yes.' Her sense of dependence on him was far more intense than when he had drilled her until she was hurting and out of breath.

Mr Paddon-Jones himself was there to take the plaster off.

'It's good, it's good!' he announced with satisfaction.

They're not my legs, Lucie thought. Not my legs.

'I've never seen a better job, if I say so myself!' The eminent surgeon stood back to allow a colleague to examine Lucie's knee.

'Splendid!' the other surgeon conceded.

Of course this was their role, Lucie thought wildly. She might have been a piece of porcelain that had been invisibly mended, but she was hopelessly flawed.

Julian's hand came down hard on her shoulder, dispelling in part the cloudy mists in front of her eyes.

The two doctors were still talking among themselves, eyes glittering in satisfaction behind their glasses. Why were they looking so pleased when she would never dance again? From the moment she had been wheeled into the hospital her case had been regarded very seriously. Paddon-Jones had been called in. She was yet to find out Julian had done that. Yet to discover that Joel in his crazy panic had rung Julian before he had ever thought to contact his family. She had been looked upon as a very special case, and in repairing her knee and the broken toes and her right leg Mr Paddon-Jones had been put on his mettle.

'Splendid!' the second doctor, the younger man, said yet again.

Mr Paddon-Jones looked up, saw Lucie's ashen face and patted her hair gently. 'Everything's going to be all right, my dear. Trust me.'

'Yes,' she whispered, and closed her eyes. Not even in hospital had she been so overwhelmed by hopelessness. '*Julian*,' she said faintly.

'I'm here.'

She opened her eyes to look back at him, struggling now with the tears. She had known him such a short time yet even at his worst, when he had hurled insults at her every day, he had seemed an important part of her life. She had never known precisely why. She did not know now.

Julian had joined the conversation, allowed now as a

layman to inspect the knee, but Lucie only heard what they were saying in disjointed snatches. There was a very bright light above her, yet the room was dimming and brightening alternately as she fought in and out of waves of deep shadows.

'Now,' she heard Mr Paddon-Jones speak, much more loudly, 'you can get to your feet, Lucie.' She felt the weight of his hand on her arm—a clever hand, a healer. 'Lucie?' he spoke again.

She *had* to open her eyes. She had to struggle to get up.

'It's a natural reaction to feel afraid.'

Lucie turned her head then and opened her dark violet eyes. She couldn't bear to look down at her white, useless legs. The skin was not even her own, the flawless skin her mother had always rejoiced in. 'It's so important for a dancer, Lucie, and you've got it.'

'Come, Lucienne,' Julian spoke to her—not as the doctor, gently persuasive, but as Julian Strasberg. She had always known he would come back.

'Will I be able to stand?'

Mr Paddon-Jones seemed to stand back and Julian took her not by the hands, but by the waist. There were no hands like his. No support, or inspiration. Without Julian she was a broken doll.

He lifted her and she stood up, somehow.

'Yes, that's it!' Mr Paddon-Jones beamed his approval. 'Walk around the room, Lucie. Easy now.'

What was happening to her. Was she going crazy? She could not move—not off that spot.

Her face touched them all, she was so alarmed. But then Julian's arm was supporting her, a stage gesture, as though they were both to walk out before an audience and she responded from long habit; only now instead of moving marvellously, she hobbled, inside ranting at her lack of strength.

'How does it feel?' The other doctor smiled at her, understanding dimly what she was going through.

'Strange.' She knew her operation had been a great success. She knew they were very pleased on both counts, hers and theirs, but weakness and panic were reducing her to a caricature of Copélia, the mechanical doll. Her legs felt withered and awkward. She repeated in a husky little voice she did not even recognise.

'Of course it does!' Mr Paddon-Jones put his hand gently on her shoulder and patted it and Julian took it as a sign to move away, which in fact it was.

Neither man expected Lucie's reaction. Freed of Julian's strong grasp, she gave an agitated little moan, turned her head blindly towards him, then released her hold on consciousness. Her slight body, abandoned, began to crumple, but Julian Strasberg, taut with strain, moved swiftly. He caught her and lifted her with easy strength while Mr Paddon-Jones cried vexedly:

'Her pallor should have warned us. Poor child!'

Julian was silent. He had been expecting it all morning. In the crisis of emotion, Lucie scarcely looked real, or breathing, a beautiful ghost of what she had been. His own nerves screaming, he laid her down on the table, scarcely noticing the two doctors, who were not a little upset.

CHAPTER THREE

IN the taxi Julian gave her an intent look. 'All right?'

'I'm sorry about that,' she said awkwardly. 'My legs feel quite different.'

'They'll do that,' he agreed. 'I remember when I broke my ankle I was mad enough to kick anyone that came near me. Even after, I was impossible!'

'It wasn't so traumatic for you. You have so many gifts.'

'I should say you were right.' She was not looking at him, so she did not see his mouth quirk sardonically. 'Therapy will make you supple again.'

Jessie was waiting for them. She heard the taxi sweep up the drive and she opened the front door and ran down the short flight of steps.

Lucie's face told her what an ordeal it had been. 'Come in quickly, out of the wind.' Jessie put her arm around the girl, a large protective figure. 'It's quite raw.'

Lucie did not feel it; she had not even bothered to zip up her cardigan. Inside Jessie peered at her, looking worried. 'You're terribly white.'

Julian followed them in, shutting the door. He too glanced at Lucie appraisingly. 'What about some coffee, Jessie? I'd love a cup.'

'Sure.'

'She fainted,' Julian explained, and threw his jacket over an armchair.

Jessie made sympathetic noises. 'Her eyes are awful!'

'Full of visions.' Julian too looked at Lucie with sober attention. 'She's been giving herself hell.'

'I'll make coffee.' Jessie said briskly.

In the most natural way possible, Julian gathered Lucie up. 'Come here with me.'

The smell of the roses he had bought her charmed the air. She allowed herself to be set down on the long sofa and he lowered himself beside her, staring at her unsmilingly. The clothes she wore were simple, inexpensive, but such was her natural grace, the quite ordinary garments looked surprisingly elegant; ribbed sweater, matching cardigan, a soft skirt in chequered wool. Always featherlight, now her whole appearance was impossibly delicate. One could well imagine her being carried away on a playful wind.

'I've been meaning to thank you for everything,' she said painfully, acting under compulsion.

'I will allow you to at another time.'

'Please, Julian—*now*!' Her violet eyes were always a blink away from tears.

'What *have* I done for you?' he asked derisively. 'Very little. I would be quite happy to do much more.'

'Why?' She asked it diffidently, because she didn't understand.

'Because you're one of my dancers.' His brilliant almond eyes were subtly shadowed.

'Are you some medieval sorcerer?' she asked oddly. 'You know I'll never dance again.'

'So? What about it?'

She could hardly believe he had said it. He, who was passionately devoted to the dance.

'What else can I do?' she wailed.

'The fact is, little one, we don't know for sure that you'll never dance again. Paddon-Jones admitted as much. No one knows just how much you could take.'

'Until I break down?'

'Yes,' he nodded, refusing to lie to her. 'You can forget you want to be a dancer, or you can try very slowly again.'

'And at the end of it heartbreak. The moment of annihilation when one leg or the other or perhaps both together decided to give out.'

'It has happened,' he agreed.

'Then I don't want to try.' Lucie had lost all faith in her physical machine. Why, even the effort of getting out of the hospital had made her heart hammer. 'Too bad you can't put me through hell again. *Gerard*,' she imitated his commanding tone, 'what was that? Just *exactly* what was that? Never a word of praise!'

'Weren't you happy the first night of *Black Iris*?' There was something almost caressing in the vibrancy of his tone. 'Didn't it mean anything to you when I told you you danced beautifully? Or maybe you didn't even hear it?'

'Probably not. You've always kept me between fear and elation.'

Jessie came back into the room well satisfied to see that the colour had returned to Lucie's pale cheeks. 'Well, tell me what Jonesy had to say.'

Lucie sat back, not even caring, while Julian recounted the doctor's every word.

'You mean there *is* a chance?' Jessie put her cup down so forcefully it was a mercy it did not shatter.

'That we must find out. The muscles tell us. I'll have the pool heated so she can swim.'

Only then did Lucie dart a startled glance at him. 'But I must go home!' she protested.

'Perhaps.' He gave her the sidelong glance he might have given a child. 'Save that for another month. I want to supervise the therapy, and I imagine Jessie will want to be in on it too.' He looked at Jessie and she visibly melted.

'You mean I'm retained?'

'Unless you have another job to go to.'

'Nothing lined up.' This had not been a job to Jessie, not from the very first moment when she had seen the tiny, defenceless Lucie. 'Actually I've got a lot of helpful ideas of my own.' Jessie launched into an account of how she had nursed a well-known athlete, an Olympic sprinter. . . .

'Perhaps you could apply a few of those same methods,' Julian suggested, an audience of one.

'Aren't you listening?' Lucie cried suddenly. 'I'm not like you, who won't be beaten. No matter what happens you go on just the same. I couldn't take it—the terrible disillusionment, the failure. Better not to try at all then have to face the agony again.'

'Who said you have to face it all at once?' Julian quietened her with a glance. 'In a word, your attitude is negative.'

'You're a swine,' she said softly.

'So I believe your best friend told you.'

'*My* best friend?'

At the expression on her face his winged eyebrows rose a fraction. 'Tennant. Surely you two were very close?'

'I can't endure this,' Lucie cried emotionally.

'*Julian!*' Jessie decided to intervene.

'In the end it's a kindness,' Julian insisted. 'You don't know, of course, but he's back.'

'You've spoken to him?' Lucie put out a hand to touch him.

'Him—his mother. I've even had calls from his family lawyer. In fact if I had another one, I was going to report it. No sense in putting up with being harassed.'

'So he knew I was staying here?' Lucie moistened her suddenly dry mouth with the tip of her tongue.

'Yes.' Ironically Julian watched her. 'Isn't it a mercy I have an unlisted phone number?'

'By the same token isn't it a miracle they didn't decide to call?' Jessie sat back looking vaguely uneasy.

'I didn't have to repeat myself,' Julian said. 'I simply said I would throw any visitors out.'

'You could too.' Jessie viewed him with an expert eye. Come to that, she should have been able to do it herself. Judo lessons had made life a lot more interesting.

'You can't want me to stay on,' Lucie was saying as though she could not bear to go.

'There's plenty of room,' Julian waved a negligent hand. 'Make it another month. You should be showing quite an improvement by then, and because I won't have time to supervise you, Jessie will have to.'

'I won't be too hard on you, sweetie,' Jessie promised, vaguely troubled by the transparency of Lucie's white skin. Always a featherweight, she was too slight for comfort.

'Just look at my legs, Jessie!' Lucie suddenly wailed.

'Stop that!' Julian gave her a quelling stare. 'Ballet dancers must be strong.'

'I had everything once.' Lucie leaned down and slid her fingertips to her toes, unconsciously balletic in her slightest movement.

'Not quite,' Julian drawled. 'Of course you came on a tremendous lot, but that was only because I was so relentless with you. You have style, classical purity, but never by any chance could I call you a ballerina.'

To Jessie's way of thinking, he was being shockingly hard on her, but no doubt he had his reasons. Indignation was making Lucie's white cheeks blossom pink.

'Surely I'm keeping you, Julian?'

'Don't be insolent,' he said coldly.

'I'm not being insolent!'

'Well—difficult.' He stood up and touched the side of her cheek. 'Rest today. Tomorrow your therapy begins.'

By the end of a fortnight Jessie had to admit that Lucie was not coming to her therapy eagerly. Her accident had been a savage blow not only to her limbs but the founts of her mind. She seemed to have lost confidence, all hope that she would ever dance again. Not *ever* on stage. Not even for her own private satisfaction.

'I can't do it, Jessie!' she cried, time and time again.

'Yes, you can.' This from Jessie, crisply. She was beginning to think she would have to speak to Julian privately. It was obvious Lucie was sick with dread even about trying, almost as though her limbs were in imminent danger of giving out on her with the mildest effort. The trouble, of course, was psychological. Jessie just knew that eventually Lucie would regain normal strength, and at this stage she did not care to remind herself that dancers needed a great deal more than that. Single and childless, Jessie had a strong maternal instinct.

'How's that?' she asked Lucie bracingly.

'It hurts like the devil.' The sweat had broken out all over Lucie's small face and she was inhaling deeply.

'Then we'll stop now,' said Jessie, 'and think about lunch.' They might as well, Jessie thought. She was not achieving much pleading and threatening. She would have to speak to Julian—the truth, this time. Delicate little Lucie required a strong hand.

Lucie was sitting up in bed reading when Julian looked in on her.

'Oh, hello!' She looked up shocked, fully expecting to see Jessie's rumpled head appear around the door.

'Lucie.' He looked irritable and moody, as if he had been through a long and tiring day.

'How did the performance go?' She put down her book, swallowing nervously. She was wearing a nightgown Jessie had given her and one small puffed sleeve had fallen off her shoulder.

'So-so.' He shrugged a shoulder elegantly but with a familiar look of dissatisfaction. 'Camilla lacks—how shall I say it?—spice, for the role.'

'Why don't you tell her that?' she asked daringly. Camilla was never subjected to the tirades she had had to endure.

'No need. She's aware of it herself.' He walked

nearer the bed, looking down at her. 'How are the exercises going?'

'Great.' Her violet eyes darkened at her own lie.

'Let me be the judge of that.'

Always acutely sensitive to his moods, she read his tone accurately. 'What's the matter?' Immediately she said it she caught her lower lip between her teeth.

Julian did not even bother explaining. 'Tomorrow I want you to come in to class.'

'Oh, no!' She made a sound of distress and shrank back against the pillows. 'I'll never be ready for class again, Julian. Don't talk about it.'

'I'm *not* talking about it,' he said harshly. 'I'm *telling* you. Be ready in the morning. I'm taking you in with me.'

Lucie drew in her breath again, ready to speak, but he turned his back on her and walked to the door. Part of Lucie sought to plead with him, part warned her not to. Not now. Time enough for that in the morning.

Jessie, a cup of tea in hand, had to call Lucie's name several times before her slight body swayed up.

'Oh, Jessie,' she said plaintively, and held her hand to her temple, 'I've got a terrible headache. I think I'll have to stay in bed today.'

'Breakfast will make you feel better,' Jessie said with a buoyancy she did not feel. 'Here, drink down this cup of tea and I'll see what I can rustle up.'

'No, really, Jessie,' Lucie held out a staying hand, 'I couldn't manage anything. I feel ill.'

She could not face class; Jessie could see that. Jessie glanced down at her watch, then at Lucie's frightened face. 'Shall I call a doctor?'

'*No!*' Lucie did not even falter. 'I'm sure there's nothing wrong with me. I just don't feel well.'

'What's bothering you, sweetie?' Jessie sank down on the bed, feeling a deep current of sadness. Pyschological damage was incalculable. People had even been known to consign themselves to wheel-chairs.

'You haven't spoken to Julian, have you?'

'About what?' Jessie could hear that faint edge of hysteria.

'About my progress.'

'He always asks, of course.' Jessie smiled at her calmingly, certain Lucie needed shock tactics but un-certain what Julian intended.

'He wants me to go in to *class*!' Lucie's violet eyes mirrored her terror.

'So?'

'You can't know what you're saying, Jessie!' Lucie stared back incredulously. 'I can't go to class. I can't possibly work out—you *know* that!'

Jessie brought her strong, warm hand consolingly down on Lucie's. 'I expect Julian has a few little lim-bering up exercises worked out—nothing strenuous.'

'You don't know him!' Lucie suddenly shouted. 'He's *merciless*!'

'He has your welfare very much at heart,' Jessie cor-rected her almost sternly. 'He won't ask you to do any-thing you're not able.'

'Oh, Jessie!' Lucie bowed her silky raven head like an abandoned child.

'There, there.' Even Jessie, normally a tower of strength to her patients, was flustered. 'I know Julian is very volatile. . . .'

'He goes up in flames!' Lucie threw her two arms in the air with such expressiveness Jessie blinked.

'It's simply, dear, that he wants to check on you himself. You know he's never home these days, so you *must* go with him to the studio. What is there to fear?'

'Ah,' said Lucie, and gave a funny little laugh. 'I can't do it, Jessie. I'm not the same person any more. Lucienne Gerard has vanished for ever. All that is left is what you see here.'

'A fighter, surely?' Jessie said gently. 'You've told me enough for me to realise just how difficult it's been—the long years of training, the living with pain.'

'I can't live without my legs,' Lucie pointed out in a tense little whisper. 'I really am *trying* for you, Jessie, but you just can't imagine the loss ... the things I used to do so easily, the unthinking absolute security, my life's work, my mother's dream, wrecked. *I'm* wrecked, Jessie. I just have to face it, and because you're my friend you have to too.'

If only I could get my hands on that Joel! Jessie thought. The expression on Lucie's small, exquisite face was breaking her heart. 'All right, sweetie,' she stood up, 'I'll tell Julian you're not feeling well.'

Immediately Lucie relaxed, anxiety replaced by a thank-God expression. 'I won't get up for breakfast until he's gone.'

'I'll bring you something,' Jessie promised.

Fifteen minutes later that was what she did, and a scant half hour after that Julian walked purposefully into Lucie's room, so vibrant, so virile, so clearly on course, Lucie saw him as a pagan conqueror.

'Poor little mite! Sick today?' he taunted her.

'Yes.' Had she still been holding her cup of coffee it would have splashed all over the place.

'Let me hold your hand.'

'Just keep away!' she said shakily.

'Stop being so miserable! You'll drive us both mad.'

'*Please*, Julian,' her violet eyes started to mist over with tears, 'I can't go with you. I wish I could, but I can't. You broke your ankle—don't you remember what it's like?'

'You're just so bloody sorry for yourself,' he told her contemptuously. 'Is this to be the pattern of your life? Lying in bed?'

'You're hateful!' She could feel her revulsion showing in her face.

'I agree. You want someone sentimental. You want someone to say, poor little darling, it's so awful what's happened to you you might as well die.'

'I don't mind,' she said bitterly. 'I've got nothing else to do.'

'Haven't you?' His black eyes blazed and he threw back the bedcovers. 'Get the hell out of that bed. *Get up!*' One hand reached for her own, clamped on it, and activated by real terror, Lucie launched her body up, surprised at the way it flew, linking her hands on his wrist, almost as though she was on stage.

'You do it easily.' He drew her right up hard against his singularly beautiful body.

'Julian!' She had to bend backwards to look into his face, the terror replaced by a now inevitable excitement.

'Is it all settled? You come with me?'

At that moment Lucie felt as though her trembling body *could* dance, he was so strong, so dominant. 'I can try,' she said faintly, not recognising the expression on his face.

'You have no other choice.' His arms were still around her—not with the violence that had galvanised her into that virtuoso flying leap, but with a sensuality that took her into an alien realm. While she stared up at him, half hypnotised, he lifted her boldly, powerfully into his arms, then brought his mouth down on hers with a sweet, savage force.

Shock waves rampaged through her body, burning along her veins. Even the instant of shocked resistance could not last. The scent of him was in her nostrils. She thought of wood smoke and fine leather, tangy blue air. Yet his skin was contradictory; rasping satin, burning hers where it touched.

She was not even aware she had lifted her arms to lock them tightly behind his head, so it might have seemed to anyone surprising them that she was the helpless victim of a desperate, sexual hunger.

Effortlessly he held her, barely disturbed by her weight, fitting her small breasts against the hard contours of his chest so that she had the compulsive urge to twist her body even closer, shamelessly inviting his electrifying possession. For the first time in her virgin life Lucie was in bondage to the frightening pleasure of the flesh. Unholy sensations that assaulted her, radiating pinpoints all over her body.

Beneath the inadequacy of her thin nightgown, her heart was as frenzied as a wild creature in a cage, leaping in agitation, battering itself painfully against the tight cage of her ribs. It could no more escape than she could. Stars were everywhere, shattering black velvet, celestial visions that flooded in on her mind while the flames continued to envelop her body. It was an experience on two levels, a journey into sensation, yet it was happening in daylight to complete silence and not the music of the spheres.

When Julian finally lifted his head, she fell back to earth, the shock of re-entry not to be endured. She only realised she was moaning when she heard those soft little sounds.

'Stay with me.' He was looking down at her, his eyes brilliant, the skin stretched taut over his high cheekbones.

How many women had he said that to? she wondered dazedly. So many in a brilliant career. Camilla. Still so dislocated, she closed her heavy black lashes protectively against her white cheeks.

'Lucie?'

'*No!*' She had to respond in a whisper, yet it was truly meant. Too much driving force would rob her of her own identity.

'You *will*, if I have to chain you to my side.'

Her dark amethyst eyes flew open and she saw the ruthless absorption behind the striking, essentially arrogant face. He *was* a sorcerer, a manipulator, complex and devious, using any means in his power to make her his slave.

She did not know why, but she did know he wanted this very much. 'Why do you concern yourself with me?' she asked faintly

'That doesn't matter.' He lowered her gently to her feet but still held her.

'It does!' She was frightened he would get such a hold on her it would be too late for anything. 'You're trying to deepen the connection. *Why*, Julian? What do you want of me?'

She half expected him to fling her off, instead he said calmly: 'You inspire me. Surely it's occurred to you.'

'I can't dance.' All at once she crumpled and sank back upon the bed.

'You can move.' His eyes had lost their turbulence. He looked cool and calculating. 'You have a quality of beauty I've never seen in anyone else—such innocence, yet a powerful allure. *Black Iris* is out of the way. I have another ballet, here in my mind.' He tapped his right temple, his black eyes narrowing over her grace-fully bent body.

'You can't put me together again. I can't dance.'

'Well then, I'll patch you up so no one but the two of us will know.' His white smile flashed, touching the hard arrogance with great charm. 'Come, little one, get dressed. Today I'll go to great care and trouble not to upset you.'

Triumphantly he walked to the door, and Lucie closed her eyes the better to comtemplate that state-ment. How dreadfully *wrong*! She would remember the first time he had kissed her when her raven hair had turned white.

As soon as she stepped into the mirrored studio, the assembled dancers broke into a spontaneous applause.

'Thank God, Lucie!' Three of the girls caught her up, taking it in turns to kiss her, on both cheeks, French fashion.

This set the rest off. They swelled around her, clutching and kissing, their pleasure genuine, because every accident robbed them of precious nerve and because Lucie had always been sweet and gentle and friendly and, to nearly all of them at some stage, that rare thing—helpful, throwing hints away where others would have guarded their knowledge jealously.

Julian allowed them all several minutes, then he clapped his palms together. 'Silence!'

They were all turned to stone.

'Lucie,' with his hand on her shoulder, he turned her back towards the dressing room, 'go and change into your practice clothes, and tie that hair back, please.'

There was something comforting about being back in the studio and mercifully Camilla had not yet put in an appearance. Lucie hurried away. No fear now. God had spared her. She was as other girls. No one but another dancer would ever know her footwork was too slow.

When she was near exhaustion, Camilla arrived, her eyes freezing over when she saw Lucie still limbering at the barre.

''Struth!' one of the boys whispered from behind Lucie. Still executing a brace of steps, he studied the ballerina's face, and he was not the only one. Everyone in the company was aware of Camilla's hatred and jealousy of Lucie Gerard, but surely now there was no need? They had all seen what Lucie was suffering on the mildest workout. Unless a miracle happened, she was finished as a dancer. So why the murderous expression on Camilla's narrow face?

'When you're ready, Camilla.' Eyes narrowed, head high and face haughty, Julian ended all speculation.

'Of course, darling,' Camilla snarled, and though many places were made for her she gestured sharply with her right hand to indicate that Bruno, the boy behind Lucie, should move back.

It was unthinkable to anyone that Camilla should try to torture the pitiably reduced Lucie, but that was exactly what she did, executing the most complex and difficult movements, holding on to the barre and letting go of it, her inner rage alone keeping her centre. Where Lucie wobbled, Camilla held perfect balance, where Lucie sweated, Camilla looked as if she had not yet warmed up.

The tension in the winter-grey mirrored room mounted by the seconds. Everyone recognised what Camilla was doing, the cruel bitch, but Julian Strasberg was ignoring both of them totally. He was rehearsing Sabrina and Robert, a young husband and wife team who had come to him from South Africa.

With Julian's eyes off her, Camilla decided to try jostling the insecure Lucie.

'Excuse *me*,' she said witheringly when her *rond de jambe en l'air* struck into the single leg Lucie was balanced on.

Lucie grabbed instantly for the barre, her mind flashing warning signals all along. She knew she could walk away. She was exhausted in any case, but the force of her own spirit held her there.

'Do you want more room, Camilla?' she asked evenly.

'I barely touched you.'

What a fib! Bruno was having the greatest difficulty keeping quiet, but he, like many of the others, feared Camilla as a woman and a dancer.

Lucie turned away from Camilla's terrible smile, going amazingly into a *plié* that made Camilla open her eyes.

'Where the hell did *that* come from?' she snapped out. 'I mean, it's as obvious as it could be that you're finished as a dancer.'

'Ah, shut up!' Short, compact Bruno was driven to interfere.

'I beg your pardon!' Camilla spun on him at speed so poor Bruno fell back.

'I said leave her alone!'

'Oh, I'm so sorry, *forgive* me.'

'Forget the talk.' Julian's voice whipped across the room, his black brows drawn together in annoyance.

Instantly Camilla turned around and began on the leg-stretching *tendus*.

'It's like murder when your legs won't work for you, isn't it?' she hissed softly at Lucie's back.

Soon after this, Lucie left.

CHAPTER FOUR

By the end of the week, Camilla's cruelty had become familiar to everyone, but what was more remarkable was Lucie's courage. Though Camilla always placed herself near or behind Lucie at every class, Lucie continued to work out as well as she was able. Only when she was with Jessie did she allow herself to go limp and stare off into space.

Not surprisingly Jessie was upset and indignant, offering to go into the studio to act as Lucie's bodyguard.

'Don't worry, Jessie,' Lucie always said. 'She's not worth it.'

Jessie herself was the soul of kindness and patience, but even in her own dedicated profession she had come across the occasional oddball with a sadistic streak. These days she was not sad on Lucie's account, for in her highly qualified opinion Lucie was making a swift and remarkable recovery. Of course Lucie could not see this herself, used as she had been to incredible feats of acrobatics, but Jessie had hopes. Quiet hopes, but hopes all the same.

'Just imagine, just imagine!' Mr Paddon-Jones said, when Lucie demonstrated what she could do. 'Of course I know nothing at all about dancers.'

'Didn't I tell you?' was Julian's only comment. Where Jessie continued to lead Lucie gently, Julian's workouts were becoming longer and harder, but not once did he mention Camilla's treatment of his protégée, and neither did Lucie. The curious part was Lucie felt herself able to rise above Camilla's hostility no less now when she was down than when she had the makings of a star. There could be no pain like the loss of her mother. The physical pain she had endured in the hospital had been bad enough. After that, Camilla's vendetta lacked impact.

As Lucie was coming down the darkened flight of stairs after class, she could see parked out in the sunlight a spectacular gold Mercedes she had noticed once or twice before. Something about it frightened her, and she did not know why. She was even beginning to imagine it was following her, and at that she would smile. She knew no one with that kind of car. Most dancers except the top-liners were broke.

Ten minutes later she was certain the Mercedes was tailing her.

'It *can't* be!' she muttered to herself, studying the big car in the rear view mirror. There was someone bulky behind the wheel, and he slowed when Lucie did and picked up speed as Lucie gunned the little Mazda that had been her mother's.

'I've got it!' Jessie cried when Lucie got home. 'He's a Russian spy and he thinks you're Ludmilla Whatsaname. Clearly a case of mistaken identity. Do you want me to ring the police?'

'Of course not!'

'Be careful,' Jessie warned. 'Say, listen—get its number.' This was rather disturbing, just as it did not seem to make sense. Who would be following Lucie, and why?

The next day Lucie found out.

The Mercedes was there again in the alleyway and this time she was ready to take the number, but a voice called to her.

'Miss Gerard?'

For a few seconds Lucie was paralysed, then she realised how stupid she had been. It had to be Joel's mother who was looking so anxiously out of the nearside rear window; a pretty woman with soft, fair hair and quite obviously a woman of wealth. The diamonds on the hand that was resting on the lowered window were perfectly dazzling, as was the double string of pearls around her throat and the diamond brooch on the lapel of her softly tailored suit jacket.

'*Please*, my dear, please speak to me.' Deep concern was mirrored on the fair, slightly faded face.

With her heart beating violently, Lucie walked towards the car. The bulky shape was obviously the chauffeur.

'It's all right, my dear,' the woman said, in turn noting Lucie's quick loss of colour. 'I'm Joel's mother, of course.'

She could not be anyone else. Lucie saw the resemblance instantly. She was not about to be kidnapped. Mrs Tennant had worse plans. She was about to plead with Lucie to speak to her son.

The chauffeur was out of the car holding open the rear door for Lucie to slip in. Mrs Tennant had already slid across the seat, making it clear she wanted Lucie to join her.

'I only have a few moments,' Lucie said, inside resisting this distressing meeting. Any fresh communication with Joel would bring back that terrible night. They had no right to ask more of her than forgiveness.

'How *are* you, my dear?' Large blue eyes were studying Lucie with a terrible hope.

'I feel quite well.' Lucie did not have it in her heart to be less than gentle. 'My legs have healed and I'm taking class again, as you're aware.'

'Your legs are really all right?' Mrs Tennant did not look down as she said it.

'All right for everyday purposes,' Lucie said quietly.

'I'm so sorry. *Sorry*.' To Lucie's distress, the woman began to cry.

'Oh, please don't, Mrs Tennant.'

'I'm such a fool,' the woman shivered. 'I've just had so much anxiety lately.' She reached inside her handbag for a deeply lace-edged handkerchief. 'I've been so frightened, so stupidly frightened. Grant tells me Joel will do nothing to hurt himself, but Joel is my son. I mean, he's our son, but he takes after my side of the family—deeply sensitive. I've *got* to talk to you, Miss Gerard. Not just for five minutes. The last thing I want to do is upset you, but I believe you're the only one who can get through to Joel. He's in a terrible state. Now that we've finally got him home he just sits in his room, brooding about the accident. He blames himself dreadfully, the way he smashed your. . . .'

'Legs,' Lucie finished quietly. 'Please tell him I'm all right. I had the best surgeon in this country, the greatest care. They tell me I've made a splendid recovery.'

'I've got to talk to you about all those bills.'

'They've been taken care of.' Lucie looked out the window because she could not bear to look at the woman's anguished face. The chauffeur was standing out in the wintry sunlight, looking away down the road.

'You must allow us to help you,' Avril Tennant persisted. 'My husband is a rich man.'

'I had no idea.' Lucie said it as a simple statement of fact. Joel had rarely mentioned his family and when he did Lucie had gained the impression he was far from happy at home. His father detested his choice of a career; she did remember Joel's telling her that.

'Joel always wants to disown us,' Joel's mother murmured sadly. 'He and his father don't get on—mostly Grant's fault, but then Joel doesn't really try with his father either. That's why Joel is so alone now.'

'I'm sorry.' Lucie looked at the tearful, flushed face. 'Really sorry, Mrs Tennant, but I fail to see what I can do but distress myself further. I'm trying to put my accident behind me.'

'But surely you *care* about Joel?' Maternal passion blazed in Avril Tennant's eyes.

'He was my friend.'

'You're so young to be bitter!' Avril Tennant reached out and seized Lucie's arm. 'He still cares about you. He loves you.'

Lucie simply did not know what to answer. 'What is it you want of me, Mrs Tennant?' she asked finally.

'Come with me to see Joel.'

'I can't. I have to get home.'

'But surely you're living with Julian Strasberg?'

Lucie now felt a frantic desire to pull away. 'He's been very kind to me.'

'Joel speaks of him as the devil incarnate.'

'At least he stood by me,' Lucie said quietly.

Mrs Tennant relaxed her grip and Lucie withdrew her arm. For a few moments within the luxurious interior of the car there was silence.

'What hold has this man got on you?' Avril Tennant asked, some dark shadow falling across her irresolute face.

'None,' said Lucie, determined not to be driven into anger. 'When I came out of hospital I was helpless, so Julian hired a nurse and offered me the shelter of his home. He's been kindness itself.'

'It's not his reputation.' Avril Tennant pointed out baldly.

'I suppose not. I can only say how he has been to me.' Lucie gave a funny little sigh and glanced at her watch. 'You'll have to excuse me, Mrs Tennant, but I must go.'

'But where?' Avril Tennant cried. 'You can't be doing anything, working.'

'I have therapy morning and afternoon.'

'You've got beautiful violet eyes.' Avril Tennant's voice dropped to a whisper. 'They look so sad yet kind. I can't believe you won't help me with Joel. He *has* to be drawn out or I think he's going to need psychiatric help. My husband is so angry, you have no idea. He has even called my son a perfect coward. I shall never forgive him. Joel is a wonderful boy. We can't all go into big business, and we have another son to take over from Grant. Don't you understand, my dear, Joel's remorse is killing him!'

'So you want me to see him.'

'If you only would!' Avril Tennant's delicate shoulders slumped. 'The relief of seeing you walking, looking so beautiful, will help him enormously.'

So she was caught by her own pity. 'If you care to meet me this time tomorrow, I'll come with you,' she agreed.

Mrs Tennant breathed a glad sigh. 'My dear!'

'You shouldn't have done it,' Jessie said over a small lunch.

'It seems only—merciful,' Lucie pointed out.

'He didn't extend much mercy to you!' Jessie was indignant. So much was being asked of this child and now as soon as she was on her feet she had to console the person largely responsible for her plight.

'His mother is terribly worried about him—his solitary condition. Remorse has put him in some kind of prison.'

'He's behaved badly,' said Jessie, brooding about what this confrontation might do to Lucie. Her own condition was none too stable; from an abyss of despair to trying to cope with a changed life. On top of that, the incomparable Camilla Price with her blazing vindictiveness.

'I can bear it, Jessie,' Lucie said gently. 'Don't worry.'

'Why don't I come with you?' Jessie offered. 'I've a terrible feeling one or other of them is going to make a scene.'

Lucie wanted to deny any such possibility, but she remembered Joel's bizarre violence the night of the accident, his mother's completely absorbed in her son attitude. She did not want to go, but she had promised.

'Are you going to tell Julian?' Jessie asked at last.

'No.' Lucie held out her cup for more tea. 'I expect he would try to stop me. He has no time for Joel.'

'Small wonder!' Jessie's wide brow was puckered with anxiety. 'This whole thing has taken me by surprise.'

In the end, because she felt she had to, Lucie went alone. The Mercedes was waiting, and Mrs Tennant took Lucie's hand and held it on the long drive to the Tennant home. It was in a narrow, secluded, tree-lined street, all the houses uniformly large and expensive behind tall, strong brick walls or spiked ornamental wrought iron.

'You will be gentle with Joel, won't you, my dear?' Mrs Tennant enquired anxiously.

'Of course.' I'm here to cheer him up, Lucie thought, looking without interest at the imposing columned façade of the Tennant residence. Curious how Joel had never mentioned his family's wealth. Life was full of surprises, some good, some bad.

The rest passed like a dream. They were inside the house, and Mrs Tennant was calling up the curving stairway in a voice full of excitement, 'Oh, Joel—we're home!'

A full minute passed and Lucie began to wonder if they would have to beg Joel to come down. Mrs Tennant kept looking upwards hopefully, something unnerving about her little smile. 'You did tell him I was coming?' Lucie asked.

'What on earth do you mean, my dear?' The pale blue eyes were reproachful. 'Of course I did!'

'Shall we go up to him?' Lucie said reasonably, when actually she thought, a few minutes more and I shall go mad.

'He's probably looking down at us now,' Mrs Tennant said.

'Joel?' Lucie summoned up the strength to take action. She walked to the base of the stairway, put her hand on the gleaming banister and looked up to the first floor landing dramatically lit by a magnificent stained glass window.

'Perhaps we'd better go up.' Mrs Tennant still stood hesitantly.

Was she frightened or what? Lucie drew in her lower lip and clasped it with her teeth. There was nothing so very unusual about suffering remorse, but Joel's behaviour was decidedly odd. Then again her immediate worry was that Julian would find out. His scathing disapproval was already unrolling in Lucie's mind. . . . You mean to tell me you went to see Tennant? No, his mother drove me.

A voice disturbed the whirl of her thoughts and there was Joel above her, staring at her with eyes very bright.

'Lucie!' It sounded like a prayer. 'Lucie, dear, dear girl!'

Lucie was so surprised by the change in him, she stood immobile. What demonic changes her accident had caused! For one thing her technical brilliance had been destroyed, now Joel stood above her like a victim of war. Truly he had suffered misery, to look like that. She put out her hand, and below them Mrs Tennant broke into a noisy sob.

'It's over. It's *over*!' Joel had his thin arms around her, crushing her. 'I wanted to kill myself, Lucie.'

'Please, Joel!' She wanted the peace of forgiveness and acceptance, not this arrested violence.

'Thank God, thank God, you look no different!' He caught her by the shoulders, staring now into her face. 'I deserved to be punished.'

'I didn't want that, Joel,' she said quietly.

'Won't you smile at me? I think I've been through hell!'

She raised her head to meet those light blue, blazing eyes. 'You said so yourself, Joel. It's all over.'

'Let me touch you.' Very gently he put out his hand, the fingers badly nicotine-stained. 'You're lovely. Just the same.' He caressed her cheek, the pure line of her chin. 'It's like a dream, having you here.'

'Darling——' Avril Tennant called persuasively, 'we can talk down here. Bring Lucie into the living room.'

'No.'

The way he spoke, so brutally, so abruptly, made Lucie recoil. 'Joel?'

'I want to speak to you alone.'

'I wish you'd do as your mother says,' Lucie persisted.

'I can't speak in front of her,' Joel muttered.

'Then come downstairs, Joel, and I'll go away,' Avril Tennant said with resigned quietness.

'You've got to,' Joel said flatly. 'I want some peace if it's possible.'

Lucie wanted to go away, but she was caught and held by Joel's hand on her wrist.

'Don't be angry, darling,' Avril Tennant was saying, soothingly as if to a small, undisciplined child. 'I have some phone calls to make. I'll go into your father's study.'

Joel waited motionless until his mother had moved

away, then his tight grip relaxed and he walked, with
Lucie, back down the stairs.

'Let's go out into the garden.' He almost pulled her
through the front door. 'Poor old Mamma, she doesn't
give me or herself a minute's rest.'

The lawn was like velvet and there were long beds
of familiar shrubs and flowers and the heavy shade of
lush trees. It was all peaceful solitude, broken only by
the sound of birds and the playing of a fountain.

Still holding tightly to her hand, Joel led her along a
path to a little white summerhouse mellowed by a
climbing rose. It was just the place for a private talk,
but Lucie felt awkward and uncomfortable, still disturbed by the hurtful change in Joel's appearance. For
all she had been through, her ethereal beauty was
enhanced, but Joel was haggard, with the wild-eyed
look of a fugitive.

'To get on and off the subject of Strasberg as quickly
as possible, he threw me out of the company,' he began.

'You mean you tried to get back?' Lucie sank down
on a cushioned bench.

'I saw him.' Joel remained standing, not even
bothering to hide his primitive anger. 'He enjoyed
destroying me.'

'What do you mean, Joel?' she demanded.

'I know I was responsible for your accident. I didn't
need it pointed out.'

'He can't have been calm himself, Joel.'

'He made me feel like crawling away.' Joel struck a
support post with his hand. 'I don't think I've ever
been made to feel so low in my life, even by my dad.
He warned me not to try to see you.'

'But I thought you'd gone away?'

'After I came back.' Joel dropped to his knees, humble, putting his two hands over Lucie's clasped in her lap. 'At the beginning I was so terrified . . . when I saw you in the headlights from the police car, then when they put you into the ambulance . . . I felt like a murderer. I rang Strasberg, and I'll never forget how he was with me for as long as I live. In a way I know we've got to thank him for getting the best for you, but I had to bear the brunt of his fury. After that, I had to get away. I had to be alone. I wanted desperately to come to you, to comfort you, but I was frightened of what I would see.'

'You didn't want to feel guilty?' Lucie flashed him a strange look from her violet eyes.

'Darling, I've been crushed by guilt. I don't know how I've survived. 'He bent his fair head until his forehead touched their joined hands. 'I can't blame you if you hate me.'

'You know I don't hate you, Joel.'

'Why did you refuse to see me, then?'

Could it be self-pity that welled in those pale eyes? 'Self-protection, I suppose,' Lucie murmured, at last. 'For quite a while I lost my grip on my own life.'

'Darling, you've been a saint!' Joel's eyes dropped compulsively to her slender legs. 'They look quite unspoiled,' he said reverently. 'I dare not ask you if there's a hope you'll dance again.'

'No.'

'Then how can you go to class?'

'Julian makes me,' Lucie explained.

'He can't *make* you do anything.' Joel pulled himself up and sat down beside her. 'God, as if we need

Strasberg!' The blue eyes devoured her full of mingled resentment and hope.

'At least I've got some of my strength back,' Lucie pointed out.

'But classes!' Joel protested. 'What's he trying to do to you anyway?'

'Don't go on, Joel,' Lucie said desperately, going back in time to that fatal night when he had been so angry.

'Darling, forgive me.' It was evident from Joel's drawn face that he was having a struggle with himself. Nothing would have eased him more than to blame Strasberg for everything. 'I'm only saying it because I love you so.'

The admission both moved her and worried her. 'And you, Joel,' she said gently, 'I'm concerned about you. You look so thin and unhappy.'

'I've been a bit hard on myself,' he agreed. 'But that's all over. Seeing you walking, and so beautiful, has gladdened my heart. I know you'll feel now you were never given your chance to realise your potential, but ballet is such a hard life and the rewards are few. A lot of us are shot down. I can't bring myself to tell you what Strasberg said to me.'

Obviously it would have made him feel better, but Lucie shook her head. 'There were a lot of things you kept from me, Joel. . . .'

'I know.' Swiftly he interrupted. 'I'm sure you never guessed my dad was loaded?'

'No,' she replied. 'Why the secret?'

'Maybe because I wish I had another father.'

'Is it so bad a relationship?' Lucie had wished all her life she had known the father she barely remembered.

'My God, *yes*!' Joel lowered his curly blond head. 'Everything I do seems to shock him—the way I was at school, the way I never seemed to measure up. The unhappiness I caused. Then when I decided I wanted to take up dancing for a career he barely managed to stay civil, as though I was some kind of pansy instead of a goddamned *man*!'

'A lot of people don't realise how physically demanding and strenuous our life is,' Lucie said soothingly. 'But that's changing. Nureyev on his own changed the image, with all that flamboyant male power and grandeur. Probably your father has never seen good ballet. He just needs . . . educating?'

'Too late to start.' Joel laughed a little wildly and broke off. 'What a joke, then—I'm going into the business.'

'You mean you're going to work for your father?'

Joel reached out to take her hand. 'I guess I've no alternative. Anyway, now there's a reason to it. I have to look after you.'

'Me?' she queried.

Joel's hand tightened as she tried to pull away. 'Have you forgotten I love you? You need taking care of. Both of us are finished as dancers, and in a way, I'm glad. We were always so damned beat, living with tiredness and aching limbs. I think I only lasted so long because I was with you. Now if I behave myself things will happen for me. It shouldn't be so difficult, going into the office with Dad and Gavin. Gavin is my brother, by the way.'

'You never told me,' said Lucie.

'I've been used to playing it very close to the chest,' Joel explained. 'Once I used to dream about being a big star so I could ask the whole family, uncles, aunts, cousins, the lot, to come to a packed opera house to see me. Those were some of my happiest dreams. I was always dancing with you because I was always sure you had it in you to reach stardom. Together we would have shared the limelight.'

'As you say, a dream.'

Joel did not even hear her sigh. 'I'm not as hopeless as Dad thinks. Gavin is certain he can find a place for me. He's really not a bad guy, despite the fact he's tried to model himself on Dad.'

'So when is this going to happen?' Lucie looked up at the beautiful rambling rose.

'We've got to settle a few details yet.' Joel paused expectantly. 'You've got to let us help you, Lucie, with all those bills.'

'No need.' She shrugged delicately.

'I can imagine where you got the money.' This very bitterly.

'It will be all paid back.'

'How?'

'Heavens, that's *my* business!' Lucie let her anger slip.

'And mine,' Joel said quietly. 'What has happened to us, Lucie, has drained me.'

It was so painfully apparent Lucie bit her lip. 'We're over it now—the worst of it.'

He put his arm around her, hugged her, then kissed her cheek. 'So now I want to give you the kind of life you deserve. I can be a hard-as-nails businessman if I have to. I'll get poor old Gavin to tutor me. You've no idea how pleased he was when I asked him if I could get into the firm. Like Dad, he was dismayed at *my* choice of a career. At least on the payroll I can afford a wife.'

'Not me, Joel!' Lucie looked at him intently.

'You love me, don't you?' he asked in an impassioned, low voice.

'I care about you, Joel,' she said simply, her violet eyes troubled.

'Then you can't turn your back on me now. That would be tragic. I love you, Lucie, and I swear I'll devote my whole life to making you happy.'

'Please, Joel, *understand*.' Lucie barely trusted herself to say more.

'All right, darling, I do understand. You want time. You've been through so much, and my criminal negligence almost cost you your life.' The glitter of tears stood in Joel's eyes. 'If that had happened. . . .'

'It didn't.' Tender-hearted Lucie wanted to spare him more pain. 'Accidents happen all the time, Joel, you know that.'

'Yes.' He pulled himself together. 'Look, darling, I know you're staying with Strasberg.'

Lucie drew in a deep breath. 'He's been very kind to me, Joel.'

'Except that he's *not* kind. One could only guess at his motives. I want to take you away from him now.'

'I have my own plans,' said Lucie. 'I have a good friend in the nurse Julian hired for me. She's an extraordinary woman, so different from my mother, yet I think of her as family, like a favourite aunt. She lives alone, so do I, so we could share a flat. I expect I'll need her skill for a while yet. She's a splendid physiotherapist.'

'What the devil for?' Joel challenged her. 'I'm thrilled to see you walking so normally.'

'I expect I still want to dance,' she admitted.

It took Joel a moment for that to sink in. 'God, darling, surely I heard your legs won't take it?'

'I guess not.' Lucie lowered her gleaming, japanned head, the white nape very tender and vulnerable. 'Once or twice lately, I thought it might come back. Julian makes me do everything.'

'The swine!' Joel glowered, unable to conceal his anger and jealousy. 'As if effort is going to achieve a miracle!'

'Happily, sometimes it does.'

'Oh, for God's sake!' Joel muttered. 'Let go, darling. Let go. Married to me you won't have to want for anything. I just know you can win Dad around, you're so lovely. I'm even glad Gavin has a girl of his own.'

'I'm going to give it a try,' said Lucy, something in her gentle manner implacable.

'With Strasberg to hold your hand?'

'You're not being fair about Julian.' Lucie looked him full in the eyes. 'He knows how much I love dancing. There's never been anything else.'

'But the agony if you fail!' Genuine concern racked Joel's haggard young face.

'Then I'll find something else. I won't be free until I know I *can't* do it.'

'So you're not going to give up this torment?'

'I'm growing stronger every day. Even if I never dance professionally again, I need the therapy.'

'Of course you do!' Suddenly Joel changed tack. 'It's just that I feel you've suffered enough.'

'I think we ought to go back to your mother Joel.'

Lucie stood up. 'We can talk some more inside.'

He, too, stood up quickly, stretching his lithe body. 'I'm sure we'll find her choking back happy tears.'

As a prediction it was accurate. Avril Tennant was seated in the living room, flushed and misty-eyed.

'It does my heart good to see you together!'

Lucie made no comment, but Joel looked happier and more relaxed than his mother had seen him in a long time.

'You'll stay to lunch, won't you, my dear?'

'Of course she will!' Joel informed his mother, not even allowing Lucie a say in the matter. 'Why hasn't this happened before?'

'You never wanted to bring Lucie home, as I recall,' a deep voice surprised them from the doorway leading into the entrance hall.

'Why, Grant!' Avril Tennant looked up startled and gave a nervous smile. 'Where did you spring from?'

'I had to come home, as it happened,' Grant Tennant made no further effort to explain. 'So this is Lucie?' He walked into the room, a big, heavily set man in the dark suit of a business man, and no one had to look hard to see the strength and the rapier intelligence. It clung to the man like an actual aura.

'How do you do, Mr Tennant?' Lucie gave him her hand, aware of the piercing, downbent scrutiny.

'You look fragile enough to break.' He held her hand gently, yet still managed to convey great firmness. 'I'm so glad that we've met at last.'

Joel didn't want us to, she thought, but remained silent, her violet eyes softening in response to his welcome.

'Have you managed to forgive my son?' he asked quietly.

'Really, Dad!'

'*Have* you?' Grant Tennant tightened his broad hand.

'There is no anger in me, Mr Tennant,' Lucie said quietly.

'You wouldn't allow it.' He nodded his head in satisfaction. 'My son is very lucky.'

'Lucie is staying to lunch,' Avril Tennant twittered, uncomfortably aware that Joel was muttering to himself angrily.

'In that case I'll stay.' Grant Tennant looked across at his sullen son without dismay. 'At least it will give me an opportunity to get to know Lucie better.'

They dined without haste and Lucie found herself, to her surprise, being won over by Joel's father. An overbearing, insensitive ogre he was not. He set out to put Lucie at her ease, in the process displaying a good measure of charm. Avril Tennant too became far more relaxed, younger and prettier, the incarnation of the perfect hostess. Only Joel held aloof, looking around the table, studying each one in turn. Lucie did not think he made more than half a dozen remarks, but at least these were unmarred by hostility. Lucie felt he had grown up in his father's giant shadow and had become sullen and resentful because of it. Physically they could not have been less alike; father and son. Grant Tennant was a big man, well over six feet with a heavy yet controlled physique, while Joel might have considered it a misfortune to be boyishly slim and only of medium height. Where Grant Tennant's features were strong and deliberate, his son's were rather delicate in comparison, an impression heightened by his very fair colouring. He was his mother's son and dressed up would undoubtedly look the debonair, rich playboy.

'Forgive me, my dear, if I do this badly,' Grant Tennant said finally, 'but I would like to make sure you don't suffer financially. It's all we *can* spare you. If you would be good enough to tell me what your hospitalisation and aftercare cost you, it would ease all our burden if I could settle it now. I don't think I need tell you, we've all been very much distressed.'

Lucie was not surprised at his offer, but she did not wish to take anything. 'You may think you have to, Mr Tennant,' she said gently, 'but really there's no need.'

'I can't agree.' Grant Tennant shook his leonine head. 'You must allow us to do this for you.'

'*Please*, dear,' Avril Tennant added her entreaties to her husband's. 'It's important to us all that we be allowed to help.'

'After all, *I'm* the one who nearly killed you!' Joel suddenly stood up.

'I daresay you destroyed a career.' Grant Tennant transfixed his son with a look. 'Sit down, Joel. You must consider someone else's wellbeing above your own, and Lucie is looking anxious.'

In fact Lucie's oval face had whitened. 'May I think about it, Mr Tennant?' she asked to gain time.

'You're going to have to decide now, Lucie,' the deep voice boomed, but he smiled, a kindly and at depth troubled smile.

'Then five hundred dollars would help a great deal.'

'I don't imagine that was all it was,' Grant Tennant said dryly.

'Be sure it will help.'

Afterwards, when Lucie arrived back at Julian's she opened her bag and took out the folded cheque, gazing in perturbation at the amount written in a bold, distinguished hand: 'Five thousand dollars.'

'Peanuts to him, I should think,' Jessie quickly put her own thoughts into words. 'If I were you, dear, all things considered I'd take it.'

'Oh, Jessie!' Lucie sighed.

'I know how you feel,' Jessie said quickly. 'But look at it this way. It would ease their collective conscience. You know how badly they feel. Now they want to be assured they can make *something* easier.'

'I don't care to be under an obligation, Jessie.'

'You prefer taking it from Julian?' Jessie looked at the girl carefully.

'Yes, I do.' Lucie answered without hesitation. 'Julian will want it back even if he makes me slave for it. I want it that way.'

'You can't afford too much pride, sweetie,' Jessie pointed out gently. 'The operation alone cost a lot of money. If it makes the Tennants happy to pay for it, I'd let them. You're paying far too much already.' Like the loss of a brilliant career, Jessie thought, her eyes kindling.

'I'll speak to Julian.' Lucie bent her head and sighed deeply and quiveringly like a child.

'Gosh! Will you be requiring a referee?'

CHAPTER FIVE

JULIAN, as usual, was blunt, barely controlling a demon anger.

'Send it back,' he ordered.

'I suppose I'd better.' Lucie's nails bit into her palms.

'Why did you take it in the first place?' Julian regarded her with apparent impatience.

'I think because they needed me to.'

'Conscience money.'

There was no answer to that. It was. She stared right past his wide shoulders, thinking for a moment that he wanted to slap her. 'So I owe it to *you*?'

'No one else.' He grimaced at her, then suddenly smiled; deliberate, blazing charm. 'Let's go out tonight. Carlo and Marianne are having a party. We might look in on it for an hour or so.'

'Do you good,' Jessie said warmly, apparently judging it safe to come back into the living room.

'I don't think so.' Lucie had a genuine fear that Camilla might be there.

'You're going, little mouse!' Julian reached for her slight shoulders, making her look up at him. 'You've had nothing, no relaxation, all these long weeks.'

'I've had Jessie . . . and you.'

'And Joel, for instance. I expect he was hysterical to see you.'

'As it happens, he was.'

'My poor darling!' Julian gave a brilliantly acid imitation of Joel's tones. 'There's not a thing you have to fuss about. Marry me and we'll live on my dad for ever!'

'I had no idea his father was a wealthy man,' Lucie pointed out.

'Of course not.' Julian agreed. 'Ethereal little creatures like you aren't supposed to poke around in people's backgrounds. His father is a millionaire many times over.'

'So why don't we take the money?' Jessie said, like someone who had been eavesdropping.

'You amaze me, Jessie.' Julian gave her a cool look. 'As it stands, Lucie has only to be beholden to me, one of her own people. We have to keep her free of Joel and his family at all costs. I'm sure Lucie realises by now that Joel is unstable.'

'Of course I'm very much in the dark,' Jessie said, sipping her drink. 'Look at it this way, I've never met Joel.'

'And how could you?' Julian stretched with real elegance. 'He's been in hiding for weeks.' His beautiful mouth twisted sardonically.

'He wanted to come to me,' Lucie said, 'but he was afraid.'

'Meaning exactly that. His fear was cowardly. He was unquestionably first and last thinking about himself.'

'Well, he's paid for it,' Lucie avoided looking at Julian by looking at Jessie. 'I scarcely recognised him, he looked so haggard.'

'But attractive,' said Julian with a mocking catch in his voice. 'I know I'm not worthy of you, darling. I know I've hurt you, but it's all over. Let the two of us hang up our dancing shoes. I've only to step forward for Dad to include me in the team. No one who sees you could fail to love you. You'll win the family over and we'll get married.'

'Stop, Julian,' Lucie said inaudibly.

'Are you sure you weren't there?' Jessie enquired, quite startled at the way he had hit on Joel's reported words.

'I know what sort of a person Joel is,' Julian said sombrely,' and I want him to leave Lucie alone.'

Lucie retreated to her room, bothered by the certainty that Joel would not leave her alone. Now that he was certain she was whole. Why not admit it to herself? Had her accident confined her to a wheelchair, as indeed it could have, Joel would never have sent his mother after her. Or was she being unfair to him, colouring her own judgment with Julian's contempt?

There was very little in her wardrobe. Why was he asking her? She was not really a party person. She didn't drink, she didn't smoke, she had never been a gossiper, or a splendid extrovert, a show-business type. All she had ever done in her life was work.

In the end, Jessie had to come to her rescue.

'What you need is a dash of colour!' Jessie fixed the girl with her clear eyes. Lucie was wearing a polo-necked black sweater with a black velvet evening skirt.

'You can say that again!' Lucie agreed wryly. 'All I've got is that silver pendant.'

'Not to worry, I've got something.' Jessie hurried off, a big woman, but remarkably light on her feet.

When she returned Lucie was debating what to do

with her hair, leave it loose in a straight silken fall or pull it back in its usual chignon.

'Here, pet, try this.' Jessie withdrew the most beautiful triangular silk shawl, rose-coloured and heavily embroidered with blossoms and sprays of foliage in the Chinese manner and deeply fringed in black silk.

'How—how exquisite!' Lucie exclaimed.

'Bought it in Hong Kong,' Jessie shook it out. 'Won't even go around me, but I just loved the look and feel of it.' She passed it to Lucie, who took it reverently and with a truly professional twirl set it about her shoulders.

'I'm not often wrong,' Jessie said. 'That looks absolutely perfect!'

'Doesn't it?' Lucie turned slowly, lingeringly, unconsciously in part. The rose-coloured silk lit the black background and Lucie's pearl-coloured skin. She looked beautiful and exotic, and gave Jessie another idea.

'What say I pinch a few of Julian's camellias?'

'Not the white one.' Lucie broke off her unconscious allure.

'No, I'll keep away from them. It's that deep pink I want. Do your hair in a low chignon and we'll pin the camellias behind your ears.'

'If you say so,' Lucie smiled. 'I'm so glad you came into my life, Jessie. I've never had a family.'

Her words spoken so naturally and spontaneously gave Jessie a rush of great pleasure. She had been an only child herself, nursing an invalid mother through all the years of her youth, then standing by helplessly when her mother finally, agonisingly died.

Julian saw her pick the camellias but said nothing. He had been right about Jessie from the beginning. She was one of the long breed of women who had truly earned the accolade treasure.

'What about two behind one ear?' Jessie stood back, considering. 'I always think fresh flowers are beautiful on young girls.'

'Let's see.' Jessie's enthusiasm was infectious. Lucie leant nearer the mirror, then pinned two perfect deep pink camellias to the back and above her left ear. Her violet eyes were wide and serious, intent on her task, so she didn't see Jessie's transparent admiration.

'I've had a lot of compliments in my time,' Jessie said, 'but now I think I'd give them all back just to hear, gosh, you're beautiful!'

Julian's expression, however, disconcerted Lucie.

'All right?' she asked hesitantly.

'Oh, come on!' Jessie stared at her incredulously. 'You look terrific. Doesn't she, Julian?'

'Of course.' Julian still had that disquieting expression on his face. 'So that's why you raided the terrace?'

Jessie gave a smug little smile. 'Well, be on your way, the pair of you, so I can make my own plans.'

'Which are?' Julian's voice suddenly gentled.

'Parkinson. He's got that wonderful old lady on tonight—you know, that actress. Must be ninety and still beautiful.'

Lucie flung her arm around Jessie and hugged her. 'I don't know that you shouldn't be on the show yourself!'

'Are you going to be warm enough?' Julian was back to assessing Lucie's fragile figure.

'I think so.' Her sweet, glowing smile faded a little. Julian was scrutinising her so closely.

'Put this around you anyway until we're in the car.' With complete and direct authority he draped his own jacket around her narrow shoulders. 'Don't wait up for us, Jessie. We'll be late.'

It was a brilliant night out, cold, but with a veritable sky full of stars. Before she got in the car Lucie looked up at him. 'Do you want your jacket now?'

'No,' he shrugged nonchalantly, so throbbingly vibrant one could well believe he never felt the cold. 'I've been thinking of a ballet to put on. One to bring the audiences in in droves. Something traditional, romantic—and God, Lucienne, you're romantic!'

'Always the mockery.' She made a plaintive sound.

'In spite of which you have some feeling for me.' He opened the door of his supercar and Lucie bent her head and slid into the chequered velour and leather seat. A dedicated car fancier could have told her it was a Porsche 928S, but Lucie, an undistinguished driver, always thought of it as a car to be feared as well as gaped at. Julian had already told her only a 'complete incompetent'—herself?—could cause it to do anything badly.

'Is Camilla going to be there?' she asked tentatively when they were well under way.

'Who knows?' He gave her a mildly exasperated glance. 'Tiny as you are, you always act heroically.'

'You mean I keep a drowner's grip on the barre.'

'Just so.' He laughed in his throat. 'Forget Camilla for a moment. Every profession is tinged with risk. I'm not sure that *La Dame aux Caméllias* wouldn't do—a tragic love story, great sets, a real tearjerker. It's been used before, but what hasn't? Ashton's showpiece, Verdi . . . Garbo . . .'

'Camilla Price?' Lucie interrupted almost tartly. 'Much more to the point.'

'Camilla, really?' He looked at her with raised saturnine eyebrows. 'I didn't realise you thought of her so highly.'

'The name, I suppose. Camilla, Camille—appropriate.' She tailed off lamely.

'Camilla does not excel in the romantic repertoire,' he said crushingly.

'She's wonderfully talented.'

'By the way. Enchanting, no. The audiences cheer, but they don't love her. They loved Fonteyn, the incomparable Markova, Ulanova, others. My mother, an extraordinarily lyric dancer. Ballerinas who have enormous influence over the audiences, something almost inexplicable, a kind of supernatural mystery. You have it in a very small measure.'

'*Had* it, don't you mean?' she said tersely. 'When are you going to accept it?'

'Contrary to what the experts predicted, you're doing remarkably well.'

'That's only true of undemanding work.'

'Then we'd better increase the pressure.'

After that, Lucie was grateful just to sink back in her seat and subside. Being with Julian was like being caught in a shredding machine.

When they arrived at the party, Lucie's eyes swept the crowd looking for the most ominous face of all; slinky, foxy, Camilla with the annihilating golden eyes. Didn't Julian realise she was still madly in love with him, even if they hadn't caught on to the idea of marriage?

She wasn't there, not seated or standing or chewing on lemons. Lucie could have laughed aloud with relief. It was a terrible thing to know oneself detested, and all because Julian had conferred on her her own ballet and many kindnesses for reasons neither she nor Camilla could understand.

Marianne came out to fuss all over Julian and say a few encouraging words to Lucie, then with her arm around him, she drew Julian away. Happily married to her Carlo, Marianne still went into a girlish dither and looked at Julian with yearning eyes.

'Little Lucie!' Carlo swept up with an absurd flourish that was meant to and made her laugh. 'You look ravishing! I've never actually seen a girl wear camillias. Very feminine.' He eyed them admiringly.

He didn't have much time for further study, for Damien, who had often partnered her, fought his way through the crowd and came to a standstill. 'Gracious, Lucie, it's not like you to be out of bed at this hour.'

'Julian said I might come,' she told him.

'My goodness, he *is* being kind to you!'

'A reward for doing what I'm told.'

'Well, if you're going to *ignore* me,' Carlo shrugged.

'You've got a dishy girl of your own,' Damien told him jovially. 'I'll look after Lucie.'

The drinks were already flowing and taped music spilled through the imaginatively decorated old terrace house. There were exotic sometimes unnerving paintings, symbolic, erotic, whatever—Marianne's; groupings of beautiful shells they had collected from the

Great Barrier Reef and Fiji, secondhand shop finds, decorative ballet posters and on an end wall, the pièce de résistance, a gigantic blown up press photograph of Julian, stunning in the extreme.

'Unwise, wouldn't you say so, with Carlo so bloody jealous?'

'What a photograph!' Lucie couldn't quite control her own lurch of excitement.

'Poor old Marianne thinks it's priceless!' Damien told her.

'Amazing!' Lucie began to laugh. A lot of women seemed to fantasise about Julian, thinking exactly what they wanted to. From Marianne's paintings, Lucie would have thought the fantasies to be somewhat bizarre. Wisely she turned her own back on Julian's Heathcliff-type regard.

It was then that an extremely elegant older woman with superb presence and a splendid head of auburn hair drew Carlo towards them, obviously wishing to be introduced.

'I've seen you dance, my dear,' the woman said, then winced very slightly as though realising Lucie wouldn't care to be reminded.

'Sarah's the fashion and beauty editor of *Flair*,' Carlo told them after the usual exchange of pleasantries.

'I know it well.' Lucie looked at the woman with warmth and admiration. 'You must have a very exciting and stimulating career.'

'I do!' Sarah exclaimed. 'But when I really start to enjoy myself is when I find a new face.'

'God, on top of everything else, not Julian!' Damien struck his brow.

'Be a good boy and let me talk to Lucienne,' Sarah said.

'You mean *Lucie*?' Damien demanded, suddenly awestruck. 'You're talking about Lucie?'

'It would be a problem putting make-up on Julian,' Sarah pointed out mildly. 'Of course I'm talking about Lucie.'

'Then I'll drag this guy off.' Carlo smiled at them both and did exactly that.

'I'll bet you photograph exceptionally well, Lucie?' Sarah asked immediately they were alone.

'Flattering, yes.' Lucie admitted modestly.

'All those lovely delicate bones!' Sarah spoke sweetly even as she was frowning with concentration. 'It's difficult to tell sometimes. I've had beautiful girls come into my office, girls who are marvellous on the catwalk who simply don't translate into film. Beautiful girls who can look awful and real freaks who can look terrific. We laugh about it, though it's not really funny if you're trying to break into an overcrowded world. I have seen publicity stills of you. You look magical.'

'Thank you,' Lucie responded quietly, thinking the only way she could ever be magical was to dance.

'My dear, I'm so sorry.' Sarah studied that transparent expression with great sympathy.

'It helps,' Lucie said. 'I try not to think of my life's work as being over, that it's inexcusable to keep feeling sorry for myself. . . .'

'I know, I know,' Sarah said quickly. 'You've had a bad experience, but so many people, not the least of them Julian, have told me you're coping far better than anyone expected. Julian was even quite fierce about your bravery. He's very proud of you.'

At first Lucie thought she couldn't be hearing right. Julian proud of her? However had this clever, pleasant woman arrived at that conclusion?

'I thought he considered me over-protective of myself,' she commented.

'In what way, dear?' Sarah's mobile face puckered with startled thought.

'Well, I scarcely know which leg to favour. Usually I'm breathless before I decide.'

Sarah faced her levelly, her blue eyes very honest. She even placed one long-fingered hand across her heart. 'My dear, it would make your heart glad to hear Julian describe how you've survived your ordeal. I'm telling you because I can see it's important to you.'

'So important.' Lucie looked down at her hands, suddenly recalling how strongly Julian had held them on the terrible night she had been fighting out of the anaesthesia. 'I can't think how I'm ever going to be able to repay him for all he's done.'

'In fact there could well be a way!' Sarah argued, her undeniably freckled face quite animated. 'Zara Blanchard,' she named the top female dress designer, 'is introducing a cosmetic line, and the moment I saw you I said to myself, it's settled, I've found our girl. It's uncanny—you're exactly the type Zara and I had in mind. We had thought of Penelope Archer, but to be cruelly honest, she's not young enough. You won't be amazed to hear models have a short life.'

'But that kind of work has never crossed my mind.' Lucie saw a friend standing across the room and waved to her. 'I may be hopeless at it, Sarah.'

Other girls would be thrilled out of their minds, but Sarah could see she was going to have to convince

Lucie. 'One photographic session would prove it. A top model has to sell the product she's advertising as well as selling her own model image. She has to be something of an actress, as well as an exceptionally photogenic face. I've seen you on stage, so I know your precious talents. You fit perfectly the girl Zara has been looking for, and best of all, you're as fresh as the product. In other words, neither has been seen before.'

'So what are the disadvantages?' Lucie smiled.

'I'm not supposed to tell you that, or you may change your mind. No, seriously, let me arrange a session for you and we'll go from there. The best laid plans can go astray,' Sarah said cheerfully. 'Only last week I had a glorious creature show me some terrible pictures. Of course she knew nothing about photographic make-up and she went to a photographer I'd rather not mention. That won't happen to you. I'll arrange everything. I love to score with Zara. We went to school together, she from the upper echelons of society, me from the very heart of the dreadful slums. Scholarship, you know. It was the sort of school that prided itself on being very democratic. There were five of us all told.'

A mixture of feelings were flashing across Lucie's small face. Sarah was cut out to sell sunsuits to an Eskimo, but the thought of being a model did not give her any pleasure. On the other hand if it paid well she could settle her debts. The trouble was she had not yet learned to live with the destruction of a brilliant career.

'I can hear the wheels going around in your head,' Sarah said. 'Think of it as an adventure, Lucie. There are a lot of people who really want to help you.'

The thought was comforting. There *were* a lot of

good people in the world, people who stepped in quickly to help.

'You're nice, Sarah,' she said.

'Sweetie, I too have had a rugged life.' Sarah said it calmly, but behind the bright twinkle Lucie could see it was true.

Damien came up behind them and took Lucie into his arms with a rush. 'Come on, girls, you've talked long enough.'

'I'll be in touch, Lucie,' Sarah smiled, her blue eyes sparkling. 'Take her away, laddie. I'm aware this is a party.'

'Oh, wicked, *wicked*!' Damien exclaimed ten minutes later. 'It's that awful bitch, Price.'

Lucie turned swiftly and there in the doorway was Camilla with a tall man behind her who looked like a well-dressed zombie.

'The very embodiment of evil!' Damien hissed. Once Camilla had physically attacked him and Damien had been brooding about it ever since.

And she *was* sinister, Lucie thought—a petite, very attractive woman, but with her jealous, vengeful nature written on her face.

'I wonder what she'll get up to tonight?' Damien breathed. 'There's one thing you've got to say for her, she knows how to dress.'

And the make-up and the dressing was a large part of her attraction, Lucie thought. Camilla was wearing a flowing silk kimono over a tiny camisole top and shaped silk pants, her long hair drawn back tightly into a topknot and decorated with some Oriental-looking baubles. Her companion clung to her as though he were afraid not to.

'Of course she's looking for Julian,' Damien said, following those boring eyes.

No, she's looking for me, Lucie thought. She did not know how she knew it, but she did. Seconds later, Camilla found her, saw what Lucie was wearing and raised her eyebrows.

'The way I see it,' Damien said, 'Camilla is out to get you.'

'What interest could she have in me any more?' queried Lucie, 'I can't dance.'

'Maybe it's a case of sexual jealousy. You're Julian's little pet.'

'You'll have to pay more attention at class.'

'So he *does* yell at you from time to time.'

'A lot of the time,' Lucie said wryly.

'I guess that's because you're so damned good,' Damien retorted, simultaneously recording that Lucie wasn't so good any more.

Lucie's pleasure in the evening was almost totally destroyed. It struck her, too, that she had best not show it, just as she never showed her fear of Camilla at class. Her days of dazzling technical feats might be over, but she still knew how to move. Damien tightened his arm around her and they began a quickening series of movements to a disco beat that finished up as a performance. A lot of the others fell back and let them have the tiny floor, and Carlo clapped his hands together sharply on the beat. Classical dancers, all of them, Lucie and Damien were handling modern with extraordinary skill.

When they finished with Lucie, the little ballerina, on Damien's shoulder, spontaneous applause broke out.

'Great! You're great!' Carlo called.

'Beautiful!' Julian straightened up and moved over to them, indicating to Damien he should put Lucie down. 'As a matter of fact, if you wanted to work at it, you could win that Dance Fever.'

'Be in it, Lucie?' Damien laughed.

'No, dear heart.'

'Why not?'

'She can't,' said Julian. 'I won't let her.'

'That's not fair, taking my partner away,' Damien protested.

'What about Sonia?'

'Sure.' Sonia swirled up to Damien's side. 'I'm dying to try out.'

'What about a test now?' Julian suggested, and drew Lucie away.

Neither of them spoke for a moment and Lucie was experiencing the unique quality of Julian's touch. The first time he had held her arm when she had auditioned for him she had been struck by the extraordinary male power, the vibrancy. She had never known it before or since, though she had heard about this particular quality in Nureyev and Baryshnikov. It was rapturous for the ballerina when it was there. But Julian wasn't interested in partnering ballerinas, only creating ballets that tested dancers to the limit.

'You're trembling,' he said.

'That was exceedingly hard,' she pointed out.

'You made it look easy. Not many classical dancers can handle modern and jazz.'

'I was only having fun.' The air was beautiful in the small garden, her skin overheated now in the thin black sweater.

'Just watching you has given me an idea,' Julian told her.

'I'm sure that's why you keep me around.'

'Maybe,' he smiled, and looked down at her with his mocking, derisive eyes. 'Surely it gives you more confidence to know that workout hasn't left you exhausted?'

She gave him a lightning glance, realising it was true. 'On the other hand, I'm shaking.'

'But then you always do when I touch you.' His black eyes were intense. 'I think perhaps you dislike—no, fear, being excited.'

'Or rather I very wisely wish to protect myself.'

'You know something, little Lucie? You will never succeed with *me*.'

'I believe you,' she said slowly, and her voice shook. 'What I don't know is, why?'

'You are in my life now,' he ran a finger down her flushed cheek. 'The first moment I set eyes on you I knew that.'

'Because somehow I offer inspiration for one of the world's greatest choreographers?'

'Surely that's a great honour?' he asked, and there was a hint of amusement in his voice. 'Why does it make you angry?'

'I'm not angry!' She swung her head away.

'Oh, don't do that.' He cupped his hand beneath her chin and turned her head back. 'It's not often I get to see blazing violet eyes. It's almost a contradiction.'

With his hand beneath her chin she was experiencing a strange, melting sensation that made her draw in her breath.

'You need to be made love to,' he said almost harshly.

Unable to deny it, Lucie remained silent, her violet eyes now swimming in tears.

'Little fool!' His other arm came round her unrelentingly hard. 'I could take you tonight.'

'Jessie wouldn't let you,' she whispered. 'Have you forgotten Jessie?'

'I wonder if she would object?' His mouth twisted engagingly. 'Jessie and I are very much in agreement about most things.'

'She wouldn't let you hurt me.'

'Why are you whispering?' he asked.

'I don't know.' Lucie tried to pull away, but her head was swimming. 'I know you like teasing. It's a terrible characteristic.'

'Now isn't this nice and cosy!' a brittle, familiar voice announced.

'Yes, it was.' Julian looked over Lucie's gleaming tilted head to the tight-faced Camilla who was making her way decisively towards them. There were lots of things in her way, but she stepped out with speed and confidence.

'I always thought this silly little thing had a crush on you, now I'm absolutely convinced!'

'Who gives a damn?' said Julian with undisguised boredom.

'I've given you half my life, Julian,' Camilla cried, all control disintegrating.

'I ache for you, darling,' he drawled.

'*Bastard!*' Camilla ran at him as though she intended to score him deeply with her nails, and Lucie hurriedly withdrew to one side, trapped by a latticed screen.

The blusher on Camilla's cheekbones was standing out starkly in contrast to her drained skin and, petite as she was, her flying figure struck terror to Lucie's gentle heart.

Not so Julian, who only carelessly drew himself to attention and put a crushing grip on Camilla's birdlike wrists. 'Please, Camilla, must you go through life in turmoil?'

'You're such a bully!' Camilla charged him, her expression ugly.

'Indeed I am. It's expected, with wildcats like you around.'

'Help me, Julian,' Camilla begged, seesawing to a little-girl plea.

'I guess I have to,' he said oddly.

'I'm so miserable when you're mean to me.' Camilla relaxed her rigid body and laid her head against his shoulder. 'Send her away, Julian. Send that girl away!'

Julian dropped his arms to Camilla's narrow waist, and Lucie was somehow so shocked at the sight of them she could scarcely move or utter a word. Of course they were lovers. Julian's hands on Camilla's white body, pouring kisses all over her. It would invite madness having Julian's love withdrawn.

'Go back inside, Lucie,' Julian ordered.

Camilla was still huddled against him, making funny little moaning noises as though she was about to crack up.

'Yes.' Lucie edged away with near horror. It was incredibly upsetting seeing Camilla in such a state in Julian's arms. It looked so natural—that was it. Julian had wrapped his arms around her body so long and so often it still showed.

She couldn't remember getting inside.

'Lucie, *Lucie!*' Damien exclaimed incredulously,

jerking her by the shoulder as she went white-faced
and vacantly past him.

'Oh, I'm sorry.'

'What's the matter?' he looked at her with astonishment.

'Nothing much. I'm tired. I want to go home.'

'But Marianne is just bringing out the supper.'

Staring ahead of her, Lucie saw Marianne and three
of the girls putting dishes along the buffet table.

'I'm not hungry,' she explained.

'Not at all?' Damien shook his head. 'Listen, kid,
there's something wrong, I know.'

Lucie still did not move or speak.

'What happened?' Damien turned her slightly towards the buffet table. He was starving.

'It's no good. Camilla told me to go away.'

Damien looked at her with disgust. 'And you're
going?'

'Ah!' Lucie drew a deep breath. 'Is it really worth
staying?'

'But you made such a good start, sweetie,' Damien
pointed out. 'Don't let that vixen slap you around. You
go off and she won't be able to contain her glee. I tell
you, she's wicked—or she's grown wicked ever since
she went on drugs.'

'*Camilla?*' That shocked Lucie into a response.

'That's the word. The thing is she always knows
when to stop.'

'I don't believe it,' was all Lucie could say.

'A lot of people do, even if no one has any hard
evidence. Surely you've noticed her pupils?'

'I try to avoid looking into her eyes.'

'Okay,' Damien said soothingly, 'but stay.'

It was a mistake. She should have gone home right away. Afterwards, when people were drifting outside or into conversational groups Camilla in a beautifully executed stumble poured drink all over Jessie's lovely rose-coloured shawl and then in an apparent effort to save herself clutched at Damien's shoulder while one hand raked into Lucie's hair, dragging the pink camellias out of place so they fell with a soft plonk into Lucie's lap.

'Isn't it time you went home?' Damien shouted.

'Oh, I *am* sorry.' Camilla swooped and picked up the camellias, crushing them up in her hand. 'These were silly anyway.'

That Jessie's shawl should be ruined! Lucie stared at the wet folds on her shoulder. Damn Camilla and her ugly jealousy! She stood up roughly, the normally Madonna-like composure of her face replaced by fire.

'Give Camilla her broom so she can go home.'

It was so unlike Lucie, half a dozen people burst out laughing.

'Oh, your lovely shawl!' Marianne had appeared, pushing through the equally distressed and entertained group. 'Let me have it and I'll sponge it off.'

'It was an accident,' Camilla said loftily. 'I was almost thrown off balance—that damned ottoman thing.'

Marianne's face twisted, but she didn't say anything. Camilla was an important person in the Company and a terrible enemy.

'It's all right, Marianne,' Lucie resisted Marianne's halfhearted efforts to take the shawl from her.

'Shouldn't you——'

'I have the feeling I've missed something?' Julian came in from outside to join them.

'I can't figure out why everyone is looking so grim,' Camilla laughed. 'I tripped and spilt a little mineral water over Lucie's itty-bitty shawl.'

'Describing your style to the nth degree.' Lucie flipped the shawl contemptuously and immediately droplets spattered Camilla's gorgeous, hand-painted silk kimono.

Camilla gaped down at herself, dumbfounded. An attacker all her life, she thought it impossible that anyone would have the effrontery to retaliate. Even Lucie seemed chastened by her action.

'Why didn't I think of that?' said Damien.

'You rotten little——'

'Company, Camilla. Remember you're in company,' Julian drawled. 'Come along, Lucienne,' he gave her a tiny push, 'you seem to have incurred Camilla's ill-will.'

As Carlo shut the door on them with a gesture of amusement and embarrassment, they could hear Camilla shouting. The high-pitched female voice went on and on, unquestionably swearing.

'I thought people like that only existed in books,' said Lucie.

'When as it turns out, they're acutely real,' Julian returned quite bitterly. 'I'm concerned about Camilla.'

'It's easier to be concerned about Marianne and Carlo. It's their party.'

'My dear child,' Julian turned his head and gave her a weary look, 'one must have *something* to talk about. Camilla will allow that tall, moronic character to take her off in a few moments, then everyone else will sit down and discuss the whole situation with immense interest. It's easy to see you're such a baby, and so sweetly innocent.'

'You say that like you might say illiterate. Or failing that, retarded.'

'Shut up,' he said succinctly.

'It's Jessie's shawl, you know,' she retorted.

'I'm sorry about that.'

She glanced at him quickly, but perceived that he was. 'Do you suppose it will leave a stain?'

'We'll get her another one.'

'What a shame,' she said, nearly weepy with self-reproach.

'Oh, do shut up!' He sounded testy and very male.

'All right.' Very deliberately Lucie shut her eyes, contriving at the same time to see his handsome profile in her mind's eye. What a husband he would be! In every respect a tyrant. She was sure now he was doing the right thing in remaining a bachelor. The disadvantages of being committed to Julian would be far weightier than all the violent excitements. Or so she thought then.

The next time she opened her eyes she was sure she was in a fantasy. A male hand was boldly shaping the contour of her breast, and as she cried out in that split second of fright and confusion, she heard Julian say to her: 'Hush, little girl.'

She put her hand over his and held it tightly. 'Oh, Julian!' Desire was driving all drowsiness from her brain.

'Your heart is racing.' He freed his hand, only to cup the underside of her breast.

'I don't want you to.'

'You do,' he said gently. 'Even if one can't fail to see you've never even had a lover.'

'And how is *that*?' she asked plaintively. Her eyes were used to the semi-dark and she could see the beautiful, cynical mouth, amused and relaxed.

'Please, Lucie. The proof is in your face. You're certainly innocent. Lovely and innocent—an unbeatable combination.'

'I'm not as green as all that,' she protested.

'And not so sweet as you were either.'

Of course he was baiting her. She drew away from him and smoothed her silky hair, abruptly seizing on the fact that they were parked on an empty allotment with a ravishing view of moon-silvered water. 'Where on earth *are* we?'

'You poor little kid,' he said kindly. 'Don't panic.'

'I'm sure I should.'

'Put the seduction scene straight out of your mind,' he told her 'This is a block of land I've just bought. I want to know if you like it.'

'So far as I can see, it's beautiful.'

'Get out,' he said.

'I will indeed.' Lucie opened the door resolutely and he came round to her to help her out. 'Take care. It's been cleared, but there are a few rough spots.'

'We could be in the bush.'

'Don't frighten yourself. We're less than an hour from home. I think it's perfect—no neighbours.'

Lucie stood still beside him and stared around her intently. 'I can see some lights just through there.'

'Another house. It's not really of great consequence. All the blocks around here are large.'

'And are you going to build on it?'

'I don't know. I like feeling free.'

'Then why did you buy it?'

'Don't be a fool little one,' Julian put his arm around her and began walking. 'You know perfectly well this is a prime piece of real estate. Look at the view!'

'I'm looking.' She rested lightly against him. It was a beautiful night, but cooler now, some flowering bush scattering its perfume on the sweet air. 'I used to long for a home of my own,' she said softly, 'ever since I was a child. It was very difficult for my mother, losing her young husband and then having to rear a daughter. We never went hungry, but there was never enough money for our own house. We always rented some flat or other.'

'At least you had your mother,' Julian reminded her. 'My parents never had time to love me. They were both so successful I saw more of our household staff than I ever saw of them. I was very lonely until I thought to take my life into my own hands. I was about ten at the time, determined on treading my own path. I made myself very busy learning everything. Everything I could. I was known as an enfant terrible.'

'I've heard.' She gave a delightful little gurgle in her throat. 'But you did train as an architect?'

'Yes, but I have a much deeper love for the dance. It was only as a young man that I began to enjoy my mother—as a woman. Of course I idolised her as a dancer. Even past forty she could drop twenty years on stage. Every movement, every gesture, was that of a young girl. Her Juliet was superb.'

'Fascinating, your world.' She could see how it must have been.

'You could rival her in sheer technique,' Julian told her.

'I'm glad you said *could*.'

'Little Lucie and her sorrowful heart! If dancers can come back from polio so can you.'

The moon was golden in the boundless purple sky and as they walked on, Lucie tried to quieten her mind. How foolish it would be to hope. She wondered that Julian could continue to do so. Her legs would never bear her like they used to. There was no wisdom in hoping.

'I'm cold, Julian,' she murmured eventually, her voice sounding shaky and beset.

'We'll go back to the car.'

'Yes.' She broke away from him with surprising agility and almost ran ahead, the taste of frustration bitter on her lips.

'*Lucie!*' He called her name as if he feared she might fall, and it made her immensely angry. Her path was littered with tiny obstacles and loose gravel, stumps of saplings that fortunately she could see clearly in the moon's radiance. Damn Julian! She should be praying to bear her burden, not hoping. A good dancer was a top athlete and anyone could see she had lost her brilliant technique. What was a beautiful port de bras when she was terrified of her footwork?

'You hate me, don't you?' He caught her up so masterfully, she cried out.

'Why do you let me keep hoping, Julian? It's a cruelty!'

'A cruelty you should be glad to bear. Where's your spirit?'

'Don't you think I long to dance?' she hurled at him. 'But I *can't*. I'm a shadow of myself.'

'A shadow that grows stronger every day.' He mastered her easily, returning her flailing hands to her sides. 'To me you are still a dancer. You reflect so much. Sometimes when I exhaust you I hate myself, but I'm not going to allow you to give up.'

'But I am!' she cried. 'I'll let *you* long for the impossible, Julian, I'm going to be a model.'

'A what?' He stared fixedly into her delicate, tilted face.

'There was a woman at the party. . . .'

'Not Sarah?'

'Yes, Sarah,' she said bitterly, responding to his tone. 'She seems to think I would make a good photographic model.'

'My God!' There was a flash of genuine dismay in his voice. 'You want to be a pretty face on a magazine cover?'

'I've got worries, Julian.' Now she was nearly crying. 'I even worry at how much I'm worrying. I owe you so much.'

'Shut up!'

'I *won't* shut up! Shut up, you say to me, as if I'm a naughty little girl. I haven't inherited money. I haven't wealthy, influential parents. . . .'

'What about the boy-friend?'

It was said with so much insolence Lucie saw red. A cold thrill of anger went through her and she threw up her hand to strike him, knowing this impulse towards violence was as sensual as it was anger-provoked.

'Aren't you forgetting yourself?' he said in a harsh, clipped voice.

'You're hurting me, Julian!' Although she had

involved herself in this physical confrontation, now she wanted out.

'I'm doing nothing. Yet.'

'You're bruising my hand!'

Julian shrugged and pulled her trembling weakly against him. 'You know what I want.'

'For as long as it lasts?'

'I could make you a lot happier than you are now.'

'That may be, Julian,' she said sadly, 'but I know what happens to women you drop. They fall apart.'

'You know nothing about the women in my life.'

'I'm sorry for Camilla,' she told him.

'You would be, though with her little sharp teeth she could tear you to pieces.'

'So let me go.'

'No. You're the type of woman who twists herself around a man's nerve centres.'

'Not his heart?'

'Darling, you're the romantic, not I.' Deftly he freed her hair so it swirled down her back and the breeze carried it around her gleaming, pearl-coloured skin. 'I like your hair down.'

'Do you?'

'I'm really very fond of you, Lucie.'

'I think you're amusing yourself.'

'Let's see.' He brought up his two hands, warm and strong, to cup her face, and as he did so the breath fluttered out of Lucie's body. She realised now she had thought of nothing but Julian's kissing her since the last time he had done so; no matter what she was doing, the magic and excitement that hovered just out of sight.

His mouth travelled slowly to hers, from her temple

down her cheekbone, beneath her ear lobe, wandering, wandering, until her senses were unbearably stirred.

'Kiss me, Julian,' she begged him fiercely. 'Get it over.'

'How brash!'

Always the mockery, the brilliant self-control. 'I *won't* fall in love with you,' she assured him.

'No. You won't get away from me either.'

He drew her long hair around her throat, then as though he too could endure the game no longer, covered her mouth with his own, not content with her softly closed lips, but forcing her mouth open so he could have her more freely.

It was yearning, it had to be. A timeless quality that gave it its mystery, too perfect, too beautiful to be real. It was like being encased in a silver dome where she had nothing to consider but pleasure.

'I'll never fall in love with you,' she promised.

'That's fine.'

It was ravishing, and moments after they were together in the car though all their movements seemed unbelievably slow, possessed of such fluidity and ease, it might have been a pas de deux for two lovers Julian had spontaneously devised.

The gracefulness went so deep in her, when his hands came up under her thin sweater to worship her breasts she arched her back for him, consciously erotic, so his muffled groan was genuinely shaken.

'I've never been so thirsty for a woman in my life!' he muttered.

When his tongue caressed her pink nipple, Lucie grew so lightheaded she thought she would faint. Then his mouth, spiralling shock waves from the very centre of her being.

'Oh, I love you!' Had she said it, thought it? It was equally true.

But Julian wanted more, experiencing a deeper, transfixing passion that Lucie, as yet, was only on the edge of. Now when the caressing hand touched her more intimately she was brought face to face with severance or a total surrender.

'Don't hold back from me, Lucie,' he begged her.

'I've got to.' It was agony to be so deeply aroused. For a lunatic moment she thought of giving herself to him, certain he desired her, but as uncommitted to one woman as any man could be.

'*God!*' he reacted to her sudden withdrawal. 'I won't let you go.' He took her mouth again, kissing her with such abandon she thought she could not withstand it. She was trembling violently, or was he? Consummation so imperative it was only seconds away.

'This is hell, Julian. I *can't!*'

For answer he groaned, a vibrant breath against her naked breast. 'Terrible—to be engulfed without release. I suppose you take nothing to protect yourself?'

'No.' Other girls had an active sex life. Lucie had only sought to exclude complications. Transient passions could only debilitate and it wasn't in her temperament to court meaningless experiences.

'What the devil do we do, then?' A derisory note in among the outraged male.

'We could go home.'

'Well, of course. A bed would be a damned sight more comfortable.'

'You don't love me, Julian.' Still her body clung to him.

'How do you define love, anyway?'

'Something more than sexual.'

'Not by me,' he assured her.

'That fits.' It was no more than she expected. Julian was used to taking what he wanted, but now she discovered she did not love him beyond pride. Pride was an important detail. Pride versus promiscuity. Julian had made love to dozens of women, including Camilla. She only wanted *him*. Which was to say, she could love him all her life.

'On second thoughts, I *do* care about you.' He spoilt it all by laughing.

'Go to hell, Julian!' she snapped.

'You don't mean that.'

'No, I don't.' She sank her hands in his luxuriant hair while he rested his face against her scented skin. 'Though I've no doubt it's where you'll go.'

'You don't know me at all, little one,' he said gently. 'The satyr of your imagination is really highly selective.'

'So what exactly do you see in me?'

'I'll tell you when you're wearing *exactly* nothing.'

'Lust has no love in it,' she protested.

'You're not serious?' Julian kissed her mouth briefly, hard. 'I couldn't manage to love a woman I didn't lust after.'

'You have a facility for ignoring serious matters,' she told him sadly.

'And you have a most beautiful body. Sleep with me, Lucie?' His hand slipped through her hair with something like tenderness.

'You make me so reckless, Julian,' she sighed.

'Darling, I'm quite unimpressed with your recklessness,' he complained. 'If anything, you're amazingly virtuous. I don't know that I like it.'

'I'm pretty impressed myself.' Half senseless with delight, she still managed to lift herself off his shoulder. 'Please may we go home, Julian?'

He looked down at her for some moments, the virulent male all there in force but by no means without a sense of humour. 'Yes, we can, Lucie,' he said dryly. 'We'll abandon the awful prospect of seduction for tonight.'

She opened out the door so the night air could fortify her. 'It's far more serious for me,' she said levelly. 'I can't fall in love with you, Julian. Not on top of everything else. Plus the fact that you don't love me.'

'I don't know what I'm doing here in the back seat of a car.' He too got out and slammed the door. 'I don't love you, Lucie, of course. I only half love you. In fact I'm determined that's all I'm going to love any woman.'

'And there you are,' she said pleasantly. 'If I'd allowed you to do as you liked, I would only finish up despising myself.'

'Oh, shut up!' He put his arm around her and dropped a kiss on her mouth. 'Get back in the car, I'm in no mood to be ticked off. Not by a pint-sized little nun.'

A pint-sized little nun whose body shook with tremors all night.

CHAPTER SIX

THERE was mood music to help Lucie prepare for the camera, otherwise she thought she would have run away. Her make-up had been done over and over until Sarah and the photographer were satisfied it would be perfect for the brand new product, yet Lucie felt so heavily made up, she was frightened to smile in case the whole thing cracked.

'Exquisite!'

'I'm sorry?' Lucie only faintly heard the photographer's comment.

'Exquisite,' he said again. 'Don't worry, darling, it's not serious.'

Sarah, too, seemed to be delighted. 'Zara called an hour ago. She's coming over.'

'She doesn't usually sit in on a session.' Van, the photographer, was now put out. He was a very tall, very thin individual, dressed entirely in black, and his irritation was obvious.

'She won't bother you, Van,' Sarah promised.

'She will too.' Van's laconic tone bordered on petulance. 'You told me you were just bringing your model and yourself.'

'So Zara called,' Sarah replied. 'Don't let her frighten you, Van. She's really a very simple person.'

When Zara Blanchard entered the studio, Lucie thought they should have all fallen back. Zara was dressed in something of her own, very chic, and despite the smile, she was unarguably what some people might have called a battleaxe.

'Hmmm.' She looked long and hard at Lucie until she was satisfied, then suggested Van should adjust the lighting.

'It's all set up,' Van said shortly.

'You can't expect me to believe you can't improve on *that*!'

The contemptuous little gesture brought Van close to shrieking. 'Don't tell me my job, darling. I mean I didn't tell you how to dress *her*.' He pointed to Lucie, who was holding her breath.

'Just bring that light in further, that's all.'

'It could work,' Sarah broke in quickly. 'Why don't we try it, Van?'

'For pity's sake!'

'Do you mind if I sit down?' Lucie asked. It struck her that she had been standing for hours.

'What on earth for?' Zara Blanchard rounded on her. 'Ask any one of our top models if they would have liked this job!'

'Lucie isn't all that long out of hospital!' Sarah delivered her own broadside. 'Sit down by all means, Lucie. Until we get set up.'

'We *are* set up.'

The rudeness and the arguing went on for another ten minutes with Sarah directing reassuring little smiles every so often in Lucie's direction. Yet in the midst of all this, Lucie stayed calm. After all, nothing was normal in the theatre. She even started to amuse herself thinking how badly Zara would come off if ever her jaundiced comments were delivered to someone like Julian. She was simply too much for Van, who had now subsided into a seething, resentful silence.

'Fine,' Zara called, when the lighting was finally set up her way, 'it's all yours.'

For nearly an hour and a half the pictures went on, with the gangly Van bent all over his camera calling for this expression and that.

'Oh, I love it, I *love* it!' he shouted.

The two women conferred and Sarah's assistant entered on the scene with tea.

'You can see she's a natural,' Sarah said.

'She *is* pretty,' Zara agreed flatly. Gifted, wealthy and famous, she was unable to come to terms with middle age. The best brains in the world were working on space travel when they should have been putting all their energies into halting the ageing process. Desirability in a woman was what it was all about, not experience and sound common sense. More's the pity.

'Great, sexy!' Van called. 'I couldn't take a bad shot of you if I tried.'

'What was it like?' Jessie asked, as she let Lucie in the front door.

'I'd never have the stamina.'

'*You?*' Jessie laughed. 'No one can take punishment like you can!'

They wandered into the kitchen where Jessie started to make the coffee. 'It will be all right really, I suppose,' Lucie said mildly. 'Sarah seemed very pleased and the photographer was enthusiastic, but I had the feeling La Blanchard didn't think I rated a second glance.'

'I expect she was partly jealous.' Jessie automatically hit the nail on the head. 'Anyway, the money must have come in handy.'

'That's why I did it, Jessie.' Lucie fixed the older woman with transparent violet eyes. 'I must pay Julian back somehow. If these pictures turn out, I could have a flourishing career.'

'They will.' Jessie pushed her glasses back up on her nose. 'The thing is, sweetie, is this what you want?'

'Beggars can't be choosers!' Lucie stifled all her utterly impossible hopes. 'I have to make a new life for myself, Jessie.'

'Just so,' Jessie nodded, 'but you can't simply leave off your classes with Julian. He won't let you, for one thing. For another, it's excellent therapy. I really didn't think you would respond so wonderfully after your injuries.'

'That was Julian,' Lucie pointed out abstractedly. 'He took me right over what we both considered the limit. Kill or cure.'

'Don't *say* that!' Jessie said quickly. 'He's really been terribly worried.'

'About what?' Lucie asked blankly.

'About working you so hard.' Jessie picked up the percolator and poured the coffee. 'Many the discussion we've had, and I advised him to stick to it. You're far, far fitter doing it Julian's way than doing it with me. When you looked at me with those big, heartbreaking eyes I got all protective and maternal. Julian is tougher.'

'I know.' Lucie smiled wryly. 'He didn't talk to me this morning when I went off. He didn't talk to me last night.'

'Don't take it to heart,' Jessie advised her amiably. 'Just don't try to cut classes.'

'Actually, Jessie, we have to move.'

'I know.' Jessie sat down and took several sips from her cup. 'Come to that, I can't even serve you any more.'

'Why don't we find a flat together?' Lucie asked.

'What an admirable idea!' Jessie was so pleased, she blushed. 'It's just that one gets lonely on one's own and a young presence is so cheering.'

'So it's settled?' Lucie asked swiftly. 'We get on so well together.'

'Very much,' Jessie responded smilingly. 'I can take on another job and still keep on eye on you.'

'Thank you, Jessie,' Lucie laughed. 'You might pass me a sliver of that appetising pie—I need building up. You might also mention the matter to Julian. I'm not game.'

'Aye, I'll tell him.'

'After all, I can please myself.'

'Sure you can.'

'So why are we so nervous?' Lucie questioned, turning her large eyes on the serious Jessie. 'After all, he's not my guardian.'

'He's done a magnificent job these past months,' Jessie pointed out. 'He's such a mixture, Julian—outwardly so self-sufficient, so definitely needing nobody, but inside so caring. I think he must have had a very unhappy childhood.'

'A lonely one,' Lucie nodded. 'He told me.'

'So now he thinks it's only sensible not to really love anyone.'

'You mean a woman?' Lucie hardly wanted to hear the answer.

'I think if your mother really hurts you, you don't easily recover.' Even Jessie breathed a grave sigh. 'On the surface Julian can be very charming and attentive to a woman, but I've a strong feeling he wouldn't trust a one of us with his heart. Even a tender, really good little thing like you.'

'I'm certain of it.' Lucie's small face was vulnerable and unguarded. 'In any case, he won't get away from Camilla. She has some hold on him, one even he can't deny.'

Sarah rang late afternoon to tell Lucie the photographic session had been a 'wild success'. She had been fairly certain of it, but not altogether banking on it. As Sarah had explained to Lucie, the camera had a very curious eye. Beautiful faces did not always project, and many a lovely-looking girl with high hopes of becoming a photographic model had to go back to being a secretary. In Lucie's case, her bone structure and personality had projected in precisely the way Sarah had hoped.

'You're in, darling!' Sarah had enthused. 'Even Zara was pleased.'

The sad fact was, Julian wasn't.

'Be a model if you want,' he told her cruelly, 'you haven't got it in you to make a ballerina.'

'But my career was ruined!' Lucie grasped hold of his sleeve to detain him. 'You know I can never come back.'

'So you're always saying.' Anger flared in his brilliant black eyes. 'The fact is, Miss Gerard, you're a damned little coward. You've been making great headway.'

'Really, Julian. I *want* to dance!' she persisted.

'No, you don't. You want to cry.' He stared down into her shimmering eyes, so she dropped her head in anguish.

'Oh, why are you so cruel to me?'

'To you?' He caught her in a painful grasp. 'I've been here all these months when you didn't have the strength or the spirit to get out of bed. So I've driven you to exhaustion. So what? I thought the dance was all you really cared about?'

'It's unbearable that you won't face it!' Lucie shouted. 'I can't dance. I can't dance—I *can't*!'

'Julian, Lucie!' Jessie came through to the living room to intervene and Julian stared at her formidably.

'I've told you before, Jessie, Lucie doesn't need a gentle hand.'

'But, dear boy, she's doing so well.'

'No, she isn't.' He almost threw Lucie away. 'Because some fool woman at a party tells her she has a pretty face she's certain she has to make it in another world. Lucienne Gerard, a model, when she's worked all her life to be a dancer, a ballerina?'

'But the poor child has been injured!' Jessie looked towards Lucie, who was now sobbing quietly on the sofa. 'You must force yourself, Julian, to look at this. It's the greatest cruelty to raise her hopes.'

'What hopes?' Julian was in a fine temper, white ridges standing up beside the handsome mouth. 'I know what she's suffered. It's absurd to suggest I don't. But don't you see, there's no such thing as recovering overnight. Lucie only needs more time. I'm almost certain she will regain full strength and control. Her doctors have admitted her rate of recovery has stunned them. Their ignorance is obvious. They don't know dancers.' His black brows drew together and he turned irritably on Lucie. 'Stop crying. I'm not so awful to you, you know.'

'Oh, you are!' Lucie lifted her head and went to spring up from the chair.

'There, look at you!' Julian cried. 'If I moved a step towards you, you'd take off like a gazelle. It's even possible I'd have to chase you a dozen times around the house. When you're not thinking about your disabilities you're eminently mobile.'

'So what *is* it you want of me?'

'My God,' he muttered. 'My God!'

'Julian?' It was Jessie who called to him as he swung away towards the front door.

He didn't answer, and both women stood helplessly as he let himself out and slammed the door violently.

'Jessie?' Lucie started to cry again. 'I'm really trying.'

'Of course you are.' Jessie stood there a little dazed.

'He despises me,' Lucie said miserably. 'You heard what he called me—a coward. Is it possible I am?'

'Dear child!' Jessie roused herself at the sight of Lucie's stricken face. 'We all know you want to dance again more than anything.'

'But I'm too frightened to hope. Is that it, Jessie? Is fear the key?'

'You must know how you feel yourself?' Wearily Jessie sank down in an armchair.

'I only know some days are agony.' Lucie stiffened her trembling body. The noise of the car engine had reached the house. 'He was terribly angry, wasn't he?'

'Angry-disappointed.' Jessie groaned a little. 'He's determined to win this battle. Determined and intent. He has a ferocious desire for you to succeed.'

'Which is what I can't understand.' Lucie turned and walked to the window. 'At my best he was brutal to me. I could never do a thing right.'

'Maybe he doesn't give praise freely to the ones he really cares about. You told me yourself he created *Black Iris* for you.'

'Even now I don't believe it.' Lucie held her arms that were throbbing from Julian's grip. 'He was proud of me on the night.'

'He's very highly strung,' Jessie said.

'Violent.' Lucie held on to the curtain. 'How could he be anything else, with those black eyes? I couldn't count the number of times he's filled me with real terror.'

'Yet he can be so vivid, so charming. The only reason I came in was that I thought he was going to strangle you.'

Despite herself Lucie burst into a little laugh. 'He was tempted, but he really wouldn't. He's just so horribly one track.'

'I'm sure I don't know what's the answer,' Jessie sighed. 'I'm torn two ways, yet it's a fact you've made a splendid recovery, and for that we largely have Julian to thank.'

'Then we'll go on as before,' said Lucie. 'For as long as it takes him to admit he's wrong.'

'And what about this Blanchard campaign?' Jessie looked up to ask.

'If I can't fit it in outside classes then I'll have to give it up. If Julian wants me to continue as part of the Company in whatever capacity then he has to pay me until I've finally finished paying *him* off.' Lucie gave a desolate little laugh.

'In any case, you've got no worries.' Jessie stood up and fixed the cushions neatly. 'I can look after us both for a good while, until you've proved yourself one way or the other. I know you can.'

Julian did not come home until well after midnight, but still Lucie was waiting for him.

'Dear, stupid little Lucie,' he said when he saw her.

'Please, Julian, may I speak to you?'

'No,' he glanced down at her briefly. 'Let me alone.'

'You've been drinking,' she uttered in a little-girl voice.

'Dear, dear!' He made no attempt to repudiate the charge, his handsome face brilliantly alive and filled with a curious hostility.

'Shall I get you some coffee?' she asked.

'Please don't fuss, darling,' he said cuttingly.

'It's no bother.' Lucie went to turn away to the kitchen.

'So sweet, so obliging,' he said from behind her. 'I like that little peignoir. Did you make it up from a remnant?'

'Jessie bought it for me,' Lucie explained gently. 'To cheer me up.'

'It's very pretty. Especially on you.'

Something in his tone made her frown. 'If you sit down I'll bring it out to you.'

'No, darling. I'd like to watch you. You have to learn to be proficient in a kitchen now.'

'As a matter of fact my mother saw to that.'

'God bless her,' he said harshly.

She saw it was impossible to stay. 'I'm sorry, Julian, we'd better skip the coffee.'

'It was your idea.' He had backed her into a corner and she felt pathetically small.

'I didn't realise you were in such a grim mood,' she sighed.

'So now you're afraid.'

Her camellia skin flushed and she leaned back against the cupboard. 'Sometimes I am, and the funny thing is, you like it.'

'Maybe.' Julian put out his hand and clasped it around her nape. 'I've been to see Sarah.'

'I don't believe it.' Lucie looked up at him with huge violet eyes.

'You never do believe me, darling.' He dropped his hand. 'I've been to see Sarah and put my cards on the table. She wasn't anywhere near so surprised as you.'

'You really did go?' She tilted her head back and the weight of her black hair fell down her back.

'Yes, I truly did.' Julian gave her an unamused smile. 'You're mad if you think you're going to slip away from me just like that.'

'But I'm going nowhere—nowhere at all. Listen to me, Julian. *Please* listen. I'll continue all my classes if that's what you want.'

'But you don't really feel they'll take you anywhere?'

'They've been wonderful therapy. That's important.'

For some reason this made him angry. 'And you're content to go on with them as therapy?'

'I can't believe I'll be whole again.' The poignancy broke through her earnest expression.

'So don't expect a miracle all at once.' He put one hand to her waist, then the other, then lifted her with incredible lithe grace so that for a moment she was lost in her old dreams. For a few seconds he held her straight above his head, then he brought her down so swiftly she immediately braced her legs around him and settled into a classical pose.

'Splendid,' he said ironically, taking her weight on his extended knee. 'It seems you can do a lot when you don't think about it.'

'Things that don't matter at all,' she said, and meant it, fresh colour suffusing her skin. 'Have you forgotten what you used to make me do?'

'No.' His face was quite still. 'You will do it again, Lucie. In the near future. I won't give up.'

'I wish to God I had your strength,' she sighed.

'Let me lend you some.' He pulled her back into his arms and she let out an audible sigh.

'Don't, Julian!'

'Then why is your body trembling with eagerness?'

'I can't help my body,' Lucie protested.

'The body doesn't lie.' He caught her long hair and held her head back.

'But it can be made to pay dearly. I think you could treat a woman abominably.'

'How do you know?' His hand tightened on her hair and his eyes shot sparks.

'Look at Camilla,' she pointed out.

'I wish you wouldn't talk about Camilla,' he shrugged. 'Camilla is the past.'

'She still has a hold on you.'

'I suppose so. In a way. I'm concerned about her.'

'I knew,' Lucie said mournfully.

'But you're more sad for yourself,' he said insolently. 'You're jealous.'

'I can't think it's jealousy.'

'It is.' Julian shifted so he leaned back against the dresser with one arm curved tightly around her. 'Why won't you let me have you, little Lucie with the purple eyes?'

'So you can rid yourself of whatever it is you feel for me?'

'That,' he said, and sighed. 'Do you suppose I want to love you? I refuse.'

'Oh, Julian,' she said gently, and with a groan, he kissed her, unconcerned with her protest.

'Don't!' She tried to turn her mouth away, but he captured it again, not violently but with a deep languor that robbed her of all strength.

How long they stood there with their mouths locked she didn't know, there was such a hunger in her that the last thing she wanted was to break away.

'I want you curled up in my bed,' Julian muttered against her parted lips. 'Where you belong.'

'Oh, no!'

Now his hands came up to delicately trace the outline of her breasts, and her hunger deepened so that it was an uncomfortable ache.

'You're heartless,' she shivered.

'You mean you can't stand it.' The gentle touch became hard and possessive.

'Hmm.' She could only shake her head under the onslaught of sensation. He was hypnotising her so easily.

'I can't think of anything I want to do more than make love to you,' he told her in a low voice, his mouth covering hers once again. 'Slowly, until you ache for it, beg me to take you.'

Lucie had absolutely no notion from where she found the strength, unless it was that soft, sheer note of triumph.

She held herself away, framing his face between her two hands and staring up into his brilliant, excited eyes. 'I'm not safe here any more, am I?'

He shook his head and his glance became hard. 'No.'

'Then I must go away.'

'You're certainly not going.'

'Oh!' He tightened his grip so fiercely she cried out. 'You're hurting me, Julian!'

'That should tell you something.' His eyes flashed, but his hold somewhat relaxed. 'Am I supposed to marry you?'

'You're not supposed to do anything,' she said quietly, 'and I'm sure that you won't. It's all right, Julian, I won't bother you in any way.'

'You've been a threat since I first laid eyes on you,' he said harshly. 'Threats are best reduced to impotence.'

'You realise you're saying you don't care about me at all?'

'I *do* care.'

'And you want to be rid of it?' Her soft query required no answer.

'Suppose you stop analysing me,' he said tersely, implying that her doing so was likely to draw sparks.

'You're an oddity, Julian. You know that?'

'Tell me, Lucie,' he invited.

'You're disturbed.'

'Hell, I know that. I've got you in my blood.'

'And that makes you angry. You want to belong to yourself, body and soul. You can't even begin to love.'

'You've convinced me.'

She shook her head. 'I don't think I have.'

'Damn you, Lucie!' he groaned.

I asked for it, she thought fatalistically, calm in the eye of the storm. She knew Julian was turbulent, unpredictable, yet she had rashly confronted him—in her own way, courting disaster.

When he lifted her she did not make a single sound. It was even possible she wanted to be carried off, to wake in the morning beside him. Possession had already begun, from the very first moment without her ever knowing it. She knew she had to sleep with Julian; it was all part of the pattern.

But at least one person in the house was not under a powerful compulsion. Jessie's rather heavy, measured footsteps sounded along the passageway, then she was approaching them, flushed from an hour's sleep but calm and smiling.

'So you're home, Julian?'

Despite the turbulence that was part of him Julian's personality was enlivened by a keen sense of humour. His sombre face miraculously lightened and he spun around with Lucie in his arms.

'Just off to bed, Jessie. Lucie is going to come with me.'

'Is that right, Lucie?' Jessie asked.

'No,' Lucie breathed, torn between relief and despair.

'*Lucie!*' Julian warned.

'I've a feeling I arrived just in time,' Jessie said, firmly belting her old dressing gown.

'Please put me down, Julian,' Lucie begged.

'No, I'm the devil come to carry you off.'

'The resemblance is quite extraordinary.'

'Dear boy——' Jessie began with the voice of reason.

Julian flung his brilliant gaze challengingly into Lucie's upturned face. 'I guess it was a pretty wild idea at that.' He released her immediately and moved back effectively. 'Maybe you're just someone I invented,' he said tauntingly.

'So you can erase me any time you like.'

'Definitely.'

'Please, children,' said Jessie, speaking anxiously. 'You'd both be a damn sight happier if you'd only admit you really care about each other.'

'Good for you, Jessie,' drawled Julian, so maliciously Lucie could have screamed.

'There's something we have to talk to you about,' Jessie told him.

'Must it be tonight?' He gave a deep, vibrant moan.

'Yep.'

'So tell me.' Julian turned and looked at Jessie hard.

'After all your kindness, Julian,' Jessie said quietly, 'it's time now to leave you in peace.'

'Look at that poor little kid,' he interrupted, looking at Lucie standing small and lost, 'what a rough time she's had here.'

'Every now and then you're a swine, Julian,' Lucie told him bitterly.

'And you're an appalling judge!'

'One of your casualties.'

'Oh no, you're not,' he shook his raven head. 'Not yet!'

'I'll try again,' said Jessie. 'It might help if Lucie and I move out tomorrow.'

'Forget about it, Jessie.'

'We *have* to, Julian,' Lucie whispered. 'People talk.'

'You're already my mistress.'

'My God!' Jessie exclaimed.

'Forget I ever told you.' Julian looked straight at the now shivering Lucie. 'Who's next on the agenda, Tennant?'

'Oh, Julian!' She stared at him helplessly, the glittering eyes and cynical mouth. She could never, never get through to Julian. Everything about him made communication impossible.

'Well, what's the answer?' Unexpectedly he walked towards her and grasped her by the shoulders.

'Jessie and I are getting a flat together,' she said poignantly.

'Is that right, Jessie?' he asked curtly over his shoulder.

'Yes, it is,' Jessie said firmly, 'and that child should be in bed.'

'I agree.' Julian's eyes suddenly sparkled like black diamonds. 'Forgive me, little one. I know you're not ready for a lover.'

'When I find one he'll be a lot kinder than you!'

'Kind . . . *kind*,' he mocked her. 'Can you be deluding yourself that Tennant is kind?'

'I think this will all end in tears,' Jessie warned.

'Tears suit her,' Julian said caustically. 'Come on, baby, be brave and let me carry you to bed.'

The blood rushed to Lucie's head, but he had lifted her cradling her with a frightening tenderness. 'I hate you, Julian,' she said carefully.

'Damn it, you *don't*.'

CHAPTER SEVEN

IN the hectic month that followed, Lucie did not know how she survived. True to her promise, Sarah endeavoured to fit the magazine's commitments to Lucie's time-table, but there was the inevitable conflict of interests. Each day came and went in a mad whirl of activity, and Lucie was finding it difficult just to calm down enough to sleep.

'Don't tell me *more* pictures?' Jessie exclaimed at breakfast.

'They want me to do all next month's fashion layout.' Lucie gave the older woman a wide-eyed look from her thickly fringed violet eyes. 'Though she's bitchy to me all the time Miss Blanchard thinks I'm capable of showing her clothes.'

'Dreamy,' said Jessie. 'When things begin to happen, they happen. Soon you'll have one of the best known faces in the country.'

'At least I'm making a lot of money.'

'But you're not happy, love, are you?' Jessie was busy putting oranges through the juicer.

'All the tantrums!' sighed Lucie. 'Gosh, there are more in the fashion world than there are in the theatre.'

'And you don't throw them, thank God.'

'What good does it do, and it's so uncivilised!'

'Is Joel picking you up?' Jessie asked.

'Hmmm.' Lucie stared ahead of her, tense inside. 'I

told him I could catch a cab, but he'll drop me on his way to work.'

'You're seeing a lot of him,' Jessie said gently.

'Too much.' Lucie accepted her orange juice with a little smile. 'Poor Avril! She's hoping desperately that something will come out of it. She wants Joel to settle down, and it seems she approves of me.'

'His father as well.'

'Yes.' Lucie heaved a sigh. 'I could become part of a rich, pampered world.'

'Only you've been trained for a hard career.'

'Please——' Lucie held up her hand, 'I don't want to talk about Julian.'

'We always do,' Jessie pointed out.

'He's putting *Black Iris* on again with Camilla,' Lucie told her. 'Public demand.'

'Great! I can see it,' said Jessie.

'I hope you enjoy it,' Lucie said gallantly. 'No egg for me, Jessie. I couldn't eat it.'

'Yes, you will.' Jessie's professional eye moved over Lucie's fragile figure. 'It's crazy not to eat a good breakfast. It's the most important meal of the day.'

'Oh, all right.' Lucie usually did what she was told. 'Why are you so good to me, Jessie?'

'That's easy!' Jessie's eyes twinkled. 'Eat up before Joel arrives. I notice when he says on time he's a half an hour early.'

It was a very different Joel Lucie was seeing these days. Joel was now happily engaged in playing the youthful tycoon, slim and compact in his impeccable business suit, driving a large car his mother had given him.

'When are you going to give up all this nonsense and marry me?' he asked her.

'I'm not ready for marriage, Joel,' she said simply, and slid easily into the bucket seat of his car.

'How long does it take?'

'The answer's not easy.'

'I think you're simply frightened of marriage, aren't you? Mother thinks so.'

'Ah well. . . .' Irony crept into Lucie's pretty voice. 'Do me a favour and don't discuss me with Avril.'

'God, she loves you!' Joel said reproachfully. 'You know that.'

'You mean she thinks I'll make you settle down.'

'Shouldn't we at least get engaged?' A much smaller car cut Joel off and he swore disgustedly. 'Thinks he's clever, but I'll return the favour!'

'Please don't.' Lucie ought not to feel nervous with Joel at the wheel, but lately she had been troubled with her old dream—too damned often. Probably because she was often overtired.

'All right, sweetie,' he looked at her quickly. 'You know I would die rather than ever harm you again.'

The traffic lights changed and they started to move again. 'We might have a little rain today,' Lucie said, to take both their minds off the accident.

'That Sarah woman is rather playing you out, isn't she?' Joel asked.

'Actually she's been very good to me,' Lucie pointed out deliberately. 'I needed the money and Sarah showed me how to get it. It's thanks to her I'm the in face at the moment.'

'I don't like seeing your face all over magazines other guys can buy.'

'It's a woman's magazine, Joel,' she pointed out.

'I wish you'd stop being a model.' Inevitably Joel

showed his jealous streak. 'It really bugs me, though I have to admit all your photographs are beautiful.'

'Maybe you can tell me what else I can do?' Lucie looked down at her beautifully manicured hands, the long painted oval nails. Julian hated nail varnish. He had told her she didn't need it, but it was one of Zara's new line of products.

'Be my wife,' Joel countered blandly. 'We're ideal for each other in every way.'

Outside *Flair*'s offices, Joel embraced her possessively. 'See you tonight?'

'I think I should have an early one.'

'Then we'll just have a quiet dinner.' The muscles in Joel's good-looking face tightened. 'Call me when you can.'

When the car moved away, Lucie stood for a moment looking after it, uneasiness stirring. Some days when she was very tired she thought she would give way and marry Joel. It was certain he did love her. He saw nobody else; no beautiful girl he needed or wanted but Lucie. His parents had approved of her right from the beginning, and she had come to like and respect Joel's father in particular. As for Avril—whatever Joel wanted, Avril wanted fiercely. Was it so bad to be loved, to be cherished? At that point always the thought surfaced: I don't love Joel.

Lucie turned around and walked into the high-rise modern building. Two hours of too bright lights and cameras, a dozen outfits in turn, then class. Oh, God, what difference did it all make!

'You're late!' Julian looked directly towards her as she slid soundlessly into the studio.

'I'm sorry.' Lucie hurried to the barre with her heart hammering. Several of the other dancers conveyed sympathy to her through their eyes. Talking wasn't allowed when they were working, and they were rehearsing *Black Iris*. From the atmosphere it was obvious something wasn't going right. Lucie took hold of the barre, raised her right arm and began her barre work before Julian pounced on her.

Half way down the room Camilla, white-faced and sweating, was practising her big solo.

'She's no good,' Damien hissed wickedly to Lucie's straight back. 'There won't be anyone like you.'

Lucie dared not look. The music from the piano was running through her brain. Such a long, long time ago she had been Black Iris, and the most influential ballet critic had called her 'sheer delight'.

Twenty minutes later it was apparent Camilla's interpretation was not fitting Julian's vision.

'What is it you *want*?' Camilla shouted, in danger of losing control.

'Anything but that!' Julian's tone was scathing. 'Can't you put yourself in part? Black Iris is a young girl, sensual undoubtedly, but meltingly soft. You're dancing like a veritable Circe!'

'But it must be different with *me*,' she insisted.

'You're infusing the wrong notes into this, Camilla,' Julian said icily. 'Black Iris is essentially virginal. She moves with a mixture of innocence and yearning. Of course I know you're several years past girlhood, but good ballerinas can conjure up youth so well.'

'Certainly.' Camilla executed several dazzling steps, then over-extended, spoiling the line of her arabesque.

'Blast!' Julian ran an agitated hand through his thick

black hair. 'Maybe you're too strong for the part altogether.'

'Nobody else gets it,' Camilla shouted. 'No way!'

'Then you'd better pay attention.' Julian's handsome, dark face was ruthlessly hard. He swung around and found Lucie's hard-working figure. 'Gerard, come here!'

I won't go. I can't go. I'm not fit for anything, Lucie thought hysterically.

Even Camilla was bewildered. 'What can she show me?' she called. 'Her day is over.'

'Like hell it is!' Damien said aloud.

'Gerard,' Julian said again with perfect ferocity.

There was nowhere she could hide. Lucie went forward, prepared to show Julian whatever he required of her.

'You're ready for this by now,' he said severely. 'Leave out all the difficult bits. Show Camilla Black Iris in essence.'

I have nothing to show. Nothing to show, Lucie thought bitterly. The pianist started again, not tiredly, merely thumping the bars out, but correctly interpreting the composer. It was ravishing, provocative, exceedingly easy to move to. Apart from the piano, it was very quiet in the studio.

Lucie is not my name. I am Ley-Ah, an Egyptian princess. It didn't matter that she could not overtax her body. Dancing was joy. All she had to do, quite simply, was portray a young girl in love. She was still blessed with her long neck and her arms and her ideal proportions. The body could *appear* to be in perfect harmony. She didn't have to attempt that long soaring leap. She did not have to go on to pointe and hold that stunning arabesque. Once she could hold it and hold it with effortless grace. Now she had to create a role with her acting—no longer Lucienne Gerard, the technician, but Lucienne Gerard, the subtle actress.

All of them, every last member of the Company, stopped what they were doing. They stood back against the barre and the mirrored wall looking towards the tiny, fragile Lucie as though their fervent wishes would support her through an ordeal. Yet she was absolutely calm, her great violet eyes, so wonderful for a dancer, transparent with her inner vision, poetry in her raised arms.

I am Ley-Ah.

I am Ley-Ah, who can never by any chance be anything else but beautiful.

I am Ley-Ah, beloved by Pharaoh.

Once she was in the part, her body seemed to float free. Her sensitive little face grew radiant and her mind, separated from her body no longer had the power to inhibit her feet. Her own physical suffering had distilled her lyrical style, made it even more ethereal, so it was not quite the same Lucienne who had danced the role before.

The entire Company saw the difference immediately. She went into her adagio, not with Camilla's attacking power but with the freshness and delicacy of a young girl. She was bewitching. Bewitching them as an audience, so they thought themselves into a dream and the elaborate pageantry of Ancient Egypt.

Leave out the difficulties, Julian had said, but she was leaving out nothing, the once dazzling virtuosity merely held in restraint. Strangely it added realms to the interpretation, so for long moments Lucie was really the embodiment of a little Egyptian princess of great beauty, a virgin, unawakened, but with her eyes opened to desire. It showed them exactly where Camilla's interpretation had been all wrong.

'Surely she can't keep it up?' a girl from the corps whispered fearfully, then gasped aloud, for as the music swelled to a pinnacle of bliss, Ley-Ah lifted herself straight up into an amazing grand jeté that was to bring her downstage to the Pharaoh's feet.

'Gosh!' The same girl clasped herself with her arms. Such a big jump could invite injury, particularly to a dancer whose knee had already been injured.

But Ley-Ah came down like a feather into a beautiful demi-plié and before the last bars of the music even drew to a close, the other dancers burst into spontaneous and prolonged applause. Eventually the pianist stopped playing and he too acted under strong impulse and shouted: 'Bravo!'

'She's better—or isn't she?' Damien asked excitedly of his girl companion.

'She's perfect!' I shall never be one quarter as good, the girl thought in her heart.

But it was long moments before Lucie became aware of her surroundings. The magnificent temple of ancient Egypt had faded along with its carved friezes and soaring pillars, the walls painted with beautiful scenes, and gradually she realised Julian was bending over her. Julian. Pharaoh.

Her disorientated face clearly showed her wonderment. 'Julian, I *danced*!' She was nearly crying with release.

'You did, Princess.' He took her hand, his strange black eyes burning with an inner fire.

'Is it possible I really *danced*?' She was shaking violently but still filled with that extraordinary surge of power. Had some undreamed-of miracle happened, or was she about to suffer the consequences, the agonising cruelty of not being able to stand up? Just a few moments of re-creation that might set her back for ever.

'Here, Lucie, let me help you,' said Julian.

'Please.' She stared up at him with huge violet eyes. Could it be Julian speaking to her so tenderly. Clasping her fingers, stroking the beads of sweat from her temples? If it was tenderness it would make her his slave for ever.

'Rosalind?' He gestured with his hand and the girl brought to him a kind of cloak that he threw around Lucie's trembling limbs.

'I'm frightened, Julian.' Now the power was spent, and Lucie huddled at Julian's feet.

'There, what did I tell you?' Camilla suddenly shouted, standing rigidly in her pink leotard, clutching her throat as if her jealousy was choking her. 'She'll be lucky if she even walks again. She was flawed, hopelessly flawed. But you wanted a sacrifice, didn't you, Julian? A sacrifice to your altar!' She began to laugh with a strong touch of hysteria.

The sound of it froze Lucie to the bone, hysteria that rose to an onslaught.

'You can stand, Lucie,' Julian said.

'I can't.' Now she was carved in stone, her small face as white as alabaster.

'Of course she can't!' Camilla cried, though several of the others were trying to calm her. 'Ten minutes and she's burnt out. Show me the dancer now!'

For an instant Julian wheeled on her and the fury that was in him radiated like a blow. 'If another word

escapes your lips, you're *finished* with this company!'
he snapped.

'Julian.' Camilla too turned to an icicle, putting her
hands to her mouth and moaning, looking so frightful
that even her many enemies were moved to compassion.

But their hearts were with Lucie. She was still on
the floor looking crushed and helpless, and now with
Camilla's screaming cut off all was quiet.

'Get up, Lucie,' Julian ordered. 'I'm here to help you.'

From being winged it was as if she had been
battered beneath the hoofs of a screaming mare. She
tried to fight Camilla's words, but they smashed into
her brain. *A sacrifice, Julian, on your altar!* What did
Julian really care about destruction when it afforded
him the gem of a brilliant idea?

The pulses in her temples and throat beat furiously
as inaction amounting to paralysis took control of her
brain. How foolish she was to think she could fly in
the face of the gods. The same gods who had maimed
her. It was a profound self-absorption, but there was
nothing about it that was not understandable. Dancers
were very vulnerable. They lived with the risk of injury
every day of their lives and Lucie still had to be considered as a tragic case. All of them stood mute, studying her acutely.

'I shouldn't have tried, Julian,' she whispered. 'The
doctors told me, but I listened to *you*.'

'So?' Julian didn't hesitate, his voice deep and blunt.
'Your spirit isn't in the same class as your dancing.
There's nothing wrong with your legs. They work for
you. It's your head you allow to rule.'

'I can't stand.'

'You can—I'm sure of it.'

Damien and a few of the others moved forward as if to help her, but Julian waved them back. 'Get up, Lucie. You're wasting my valuable time.'

Lucie's sensitive mouth moved soundlessly in her white face.

Julian frowned, his nostrils flaring. 'Do you want me to call a psychiatrist?'

'B——' Damien mumbled.

'Well?'

The old dull gold-coloured cloak fell smoothly around her shoulders, hiding her body, but there was no way she could disguise the fear in her eyes so that those she had been so generous to in their training wanted to kill Julian for his cruelty. Now that their minds were clearer they remembered the extent of Lucie's injuries. They even remembered the story of how a swan sang before it died. For a short time Lucie had held them spellbound, now they all feared she might have done herself irreparable harm.

'Don't listen to anyone but me,' Julian told her. 'You have the power to do anything you like. Be grateful for it.'

But to Lucie, both power and Julian had forsaken her. It was Camilla who had accomplished a great deal, filling Lucie with fear so that her body told itself it could take no more hurt. She tried to get up, failed, then fell back in a dead faint to the floor.

For a week she refused to see anyone but Jessie.

'You can't keep this up, dear,' Jessie told her worriedly. 'You've got to face it and lick it. Someone is always ringing up. Sarah is just so disappointed. She's built her whole campaign around you.'

'And I don't like being a model one little bit.'

'Shall I pass it on to Sarah?' Jessie asked.

Lucie made a face and shook her head. 'I don't care to think what would happen to me without you and Sarah—you because you're always in my corner, Sarah because she's offered me the chance of making real money.'

'And do you mean to do nothing about Joel?'

'Joel—what a bore!' groaned Lucie.

'Would you speak to a friend of mine?' Jessie asked.

'I can't, Jessie.' Lucie looked away and out of the plate glass window. A jacaranda was just coming into flower. 'I'm pretty sure he's a shrink.'

'He's a psychiatrist,' Jessie explained, 'a good one. Don't be alarmed by a word. You need someone to talk to besides me, someone professional. Everything has been too much for you—the accident, more especially Joel's defection.'

'Don't leave out Julian,' Lucie said bitterly. 'Julian, my torment.'

Not for the first time Jessie sighed deeply. Julian didn't know when to give in, but it seemed Lucie did. Her experience of a week ago had caused her to go right back into her shell. More, it had broken her nerve. Perhaps even more than physically, Lucie had been emotionally scarred. 'Tom Herrington is a good man,' Jessie persisted calmly, 'right at the top of his profession. You need someone completely outside your own world, someone trained to listen and help people sort out their problems. Tom has young daughters of his own. You can trust him. . . .'

'The last thing I want to do is trust anyone.' Lucie passed her cup to Jessie for more coffee. 'It can be devastating.'

'You mean you trusted Julian?' Jessie asked quietly.
'With my life.'

'So how has he harmed you?' Jessie questioned with a good deal of feeling.

'He pushed me with all his might!' Lucie cried out even more passionately. 'He didn't care if I toppled over. He didn't care if I ever danced again. He's never had any real sympathy for me. He told me himself I inspired him—that's the only thing that held him. Ideas, and to hell with who gets hurt.'

'Lucie, Lucie!' Jessie muttered in dismay.

'I'm sorry.' Lucie put her head right down until it rested on her knees. 'What's the matter with me, Jessie? It seems to me I'm on the verge of a breakdown.'

'Dear child!' Rather awkwardly, Jessie scrambled over to her. Very gently she eased the girl up, then covered one slender trembling hand with her own broad yet very special hand. 'The simple truth is you've been through too much. You're twenty-two years of age, yet you've known tragedy. You lost the mother you adored, then when you'd scarcely recovered you suffered a serious accident. I see clearly now that it's all been too much. I know you think you hate Julian. . . .'

'I *do*,' Lucie whispered softly.

'But in his own way he was extraordinarily kind to you. Not only that, Lucie, he was the one who actually put the strength back into your limbs.'

'He dragged me to class!' Lucie protested.

Jessie strove to ignore the vehemence. It was so unlike gentle Lucie, yet her huge violet eyes were spilling fire. These days Julian was the devil incarnate, a demon who created idols only to destroy them.

'Please see Tom Herrington for me,' Jessie said in a low, persuading voice.

'How can he help me, Jessie?' Lucie asked. 'How can he understand that I've simply lost my nerve?'

'Sure he'll understand that, Lucie.'

'Nothing is going to make me dance again.'

'You're afraid in case you fall,' suggested Jessie.

'Yes.'

'Then you must put dancing altogether out of your mind.'

'That would be lovely if I could,' Lucie sighed.

'I don't wonder—it's been your whole life. Maybe you should go away, take a trip—a whole change of scene.'

'Lucie nodded and frowned. 'That's what Joel said, only he suggested a honeymoon. He loves me, don't you think, Jessie?'

Jessie glanced at Lucie's solemn little profile and cleared her throat. 'The question is, Lucie, do you love him?'

'I think the least I can do is marry him. I'll tell him we're getting engaged.'

Jessie bit her lip, looking sad and concerned. 'You're in no fit state to make important decisions.'

'Isn't that the truth!' A wry smile momentarily lit Lucie's face. 'I really love you, Jessie. You're the only family I have.'

'Then you'll see Tom—will you?'

'If you think he can help.' To please Jessie, Lucie agreed. Jessie had taken such good care of her. She was so kind and loving by nature. She would have made a wonderful wife and mother, yet her sense of duty had left her with little choice. 'You know, Jessie,'

Lucie said quietly, 'I'm only twenty-two, yet I fell like an old, old woman.'

'Then we can't delay any longer.' Jessie stood up purposefully and walked to the phone. 'You have to see Tom.'

'God help me,' said Lucie, and blew Jessie a kiss.

Doctor Tom Herrington was a tall man of about fifty, grey-haired and grey-eyed, who gave the instant impression of being both strong and full of compassion for his fellow man.

'Please, *Lucie*, may I?' He inclined his head towards a chair, then took his place on the other side of the desk. 'Jessie has spoken to me about you. 'We're old friends.'

'And a very good friend she is to me,' Lucie said shyly. 'It's really for Jessie I've come, Doctor.'

'Not for yourself?'

'I have my own diagnosis. I've simply lost my nerve.'

'I understand, but you've come to me here to find out why.'

'I can't possibly dance again,' Lucie explained, fixing him with great violet eyes.

'From what I've heard, there is no great reason why you can't.' The grey eyes were gentle but intensely interested.

'It's even a little obscure to me,' Lucie sighed. 'I suppose I'm like a trapeze artist who's fallen. I'm frightened to go up again.'

'Indeed, and it takes a tremendous effort to do so, but first I want you to bring out all your little fears.

It's a matter of talking things over, and I will listen closely.'

'I think what I'm really frightened of is a person,' Lucie explained.

'A *person*?' The doctor stared openly, but he did not appear astonished.

'Yes.' Lucie bent her head and hesitated.

'I see. It goes deep.'

'Yes.' Lucie sighed again. 'My enemy is a ruthless person.'

'So, you must tell me.'

And because she didn't seem to have a choice, Lucie began to speak.

When Joel heard she was seeing a psychiatrist he nearly jumped out of his seat.

'For God's sake, why?'

'Simple. I need a trained professional to talk to. I've been tying myself in knots.'

'But a psychiatrist?' Joel's thin cheeks flushed. They were having dinner in a restaurant, and what kind of a subject was that to introduce anyway? Or so Lucie thought.

'Why not? Don't you believe in them?'

'Darling, what do you need one for?' Joel shook his head. 'It's that Jessie, isn't it? Not a bad old girl as old maids go, but basically interfering.'

'Please don't insult Jessie.' Lucie's sweet voice suddenly hardened. 'Jessie is my friend.'

'And so, darling, am I.' Joel reached across the cir-cular table and took her hand. 'I've been so worried about you, but I'm quite sure you don't need a psy-chiatrist. That in itself is an insult.'

'I doubt it,' said Lucie. 'He's helped me already. I can master this trauma. I may even come out of it a better person.'

'Typical psychiatric talk! Traumas and neuroses and God knows what else. You've simply had an excessive amount of suffering, and that devil Strasberg has been a bad influence, driving you into the ground.'

'Please, don't let's talk about Julian.' For an instant Lucie's small face looked frantic.

'I think perhaps it's he who's really to blame.' Joel leaned towards her, his blue eyes intense. 'All he cares about is *his* work, to the exclusion of everything and everyone else. So he's brilliant, so what? I hate him for what he's done to you.'

'But you've always hated him, haven't you?' Lucie interrupted abruptly. 'For your own reasons, Joel.'

Joel sat perfectly still, arrested by her tone. She was an amazing contradiction and her feelings about Julian Strasberg were extremely complex.

'Let's forget him!' he said with the sense to hide his complete exasperation. 'You look so beautiful tonight. Your dress is the exact colour of your eyes.'

'One of the Blanchard collection.' Lucie looked down at her extravagantly pretty short evening dress. It was probably the most sophisticated dress she had ever worn and it enhanced her beauty to a degree she wasn't even aware of. It was also, with its tiny, strapless top, nipped-in waist and tiered skirt, extremely seductive, but her new, sexy looks meant nothing to her. They were simply part of a new image, a new life. 'At least I can show clothes,' she said wryly, 'thank the Lord!'

Joel did not have the chance to reply. The owner of the restaurant, an exclusive one, was greeting a party of new arrivals warmly, his deep, resonant Italian voice ringing out. 'Welcome, welcome . . .!'

'God in Heaven!' Joel muttered, and broke off.

'What is it?' Lucie turned her head and all the colour in her face drained away. 'I have to go, Joel.'

He reacted swiftly. 'I understand. But we can't leave now. Wait until they're seated.'

'I can't wait.' Lucie leapt up and found herself face to face with Julian.

'Oh!' She could not prevent her voice from breaking. Only Julian's imperious dark face was in focus, the rest of the group swam.

'Lucienne.' He nodded his head curtly.

'Aren't you going to introduce us?' A woman with blonde hair clasped his arm tightly.

'No, I'm not,' he returned bluntly.

'But, Julian darling, you must—I beg of you.' The blonde gave a little mocking gurgle in her throat.

The others in the party looked curiously, then moved down the aisle to their table and Joel, belatedly, jumped to his feet, a cold glint in his eyes. 'Move on, Strasberg.'

'Of course.' Julian smiled contemptuously. 'Frankly I don't know how I stopped.'

'I *hate* him!' Joel muttered audibly when Julian had passed. 'His arrogance is intolerable. Bloody foreigner!'

'May we go?' Lucie was still standing with the alert grace of a gazelle.

'Why the hell should we? I haven't even had my dinner.'

'Then I'll go myself.' Lucie flew away from the table without another word.

When Joel caught her outside, he swung her around roughly. 'Is he *always* going to haunt you?' he demanded.

'Probably to the day I die.'

'*Why?*' Joel could feel the jealous rage mount in him. 'You've told me you were finished with him—dancing, everything. Not once, but many times. Was it all a lie?'

'You're hurting me, Joel,' Lucie said in a low voice.

'That's another thing, you *like* getting hurt.' His blue eyes blazed with an intense sexual jealousy.

'Please take your hands off me,' Lucie said, summoning up all her courage. 'I'm sorry if I'm acting foolishly, but I have to leave.'

'It's Strasberg all the time, isn't it?' Joel shouted. He pulled her into his arms abruptly and his eyes had a dangerous gleam. 'The little virgin with me, but I bet you were ready for Strasberg—day or night!'

His strength, bolstered by fury, was too much for Lucie, but then a tall figure seemed to spring out of the shadows, took Joel by the shoulder and almost threw him sideways.

'You bastard!' Joel roared as Julian loomed over him.

'How about Mr Strasberg?'

Lucie ran for safety. A cruising taxi decided her, but as she slid in, her heart pounding, she was literally hauled from the seat.

'What's goin' on here?' the driver demanded.

'Just the usual.' Julian shoved a note into his hand. 'A lovers' tiff.'

'Then leave me out of it.'

'Thanks.' Holding Lucie with his left arm, Julian slammed the door.

By some miracle she didn't faint though she twisted and turned with desperation.

'You have to be awfully careful who you associate with,' Julian gritted through his teeth.

'What have you done to Joel?' she demanded.

'I haven't killed him.'

'Where *is* he?' she cried jerkily.

'I would say dealing with a bloody nose.'

'You beast!'

'I have been for quite some time. Serve the little rat right.'

'I hope he brings an assault charge against you!' she said furiously.

'In reward for rescuing you.' He was half walking, half lifting her towards his car.

'What are you doing?' The idea of screaming floated into her mind.

'I'm taking you home. No trouble at all.'

'I won't go, Julian.'

'What a bore!' he drawled.

Lucie turned up her face and her eyes swam with tears. 'This is unendurable, Julian. Won't you leave me alone?'

'So you can ruin your life with Tennant?'

'At least he doesn't dominate me completely.'

'But damn it all, Lucie, I don't dominate you in any real sense. You're infinitely gifted, your own person.'

'I'm just a child afraid of monsters,' she said faintly.

'And I'm the monster?'

'More or less.'

'It's a high price to pay for returning you to your own world.'

'That's another terrible thing about you—you won't face facts.'

'No, Lucie,' he said quietly. 'It's you who's turning away from reality. Calling me a monster isn't making any sense. I haven't abandoned you. You've abandoned me—more importantly, yourself. If I leave you alone, you'll become permanently fixated that you can't dance.'

It was a conflict that could never be resolved. Lucie threw up her arms in an attitude of despair and Julian closed in on her swiftly and lifted her into his car.

She did not go willingly, neither did she offer resistance. There hadn't been a day when she had not had to chase the thought of Julian from her mind. He was too dominant, too strong for her, and maybe when he had her he would stop this painful conquest. It was better to have it all over.

When they arrived at his house, he helped her out but held her arm, the tension that was in him tingeing his face with bitterness.

'Joel may follow us here,' she said.

He smiled, but his eyes were arrogant and full of menace. 'Joel has a tendency to disappear when there's trouble.'

'He wants to marry me.'

'No wonder you're worried!' Still with his hand on her, he found the front door key and opened the door.

'Your friends must find you unusual . . . unpredictable.'

'I suppose so.' He flicked a switch and light flooded down on them. 'It's not really of great consequence to me whether they understand me or not. I saw you rush out and I saw Tennant's face when he followed you. I made my apologies quickly and left.'

'And how long have you known the blonde lady?'

He smiled with irony. 'I don't know that it's any of your business.'

'I realise that.' Lucie mustered her own little smile. 'You've impressed on me that you don't have to explain yourself to anybody.'

'Come and sit down,' he said, his black eyes raking her face and her bare shoulders. 'I don't propose raping you, if that's what you're afraid of.'

'I'm *not* afraid,' she said tautly. 'I do abhor the way you do this sort of thing.'

'What sort of thing?' He was frowning, thoughtful.

'Oh, abductions.' She gestured gracefully.

'I only want to talk to you, Lucie.'

'Marvellous—*talk*!' She sat down on the sofa in a dense cloud of excitement and despair.

'I'll take you back to Jessie whenever you like,' said Julian.

'Oh, quick, quick, let's go now!' She jumped up again and made a run for the door.

'Lucie, Lucie!' He had his arms around her and her name seemed to be rasped from his throat.

'Why don't you take me and get it over?' The sound of her laugh was overlaid by a sob.

'Would I hurt you—*would* I?'

'Yes, you would.'

'You little fool!' he said contemptuously. 'I'm sick to death of your stupidity. Do you think I need a woman so much I can't keep my hands off her?'

'It looks like it to me,' she retorted bitterly.

The strong arms that had pinned her flung them-

selves away and Lucie so abruptly released, found that
her legs were buckling under her. She swayed, put out
a hand and Julian grasped her once more, refuting his
own denials, his mouth already claiming hers.

It was too late then for both of them, frustrated passions rising in a fury, overriding the defence mech-
anisms that in saner moments kept their desires
masked.

Lucie felt the hard, lithe body against hers and
revelled in the shock of it, the enormous pleasure she
was always struggling to suppress. Whatever her
separate thoughts, her body was as one with Julian's.
Physically he was perfect to her, his hands, his mouth,
the hard muscles rippling smoothly beneath her
fingers.

That he could bring her such joy was the source of
her nightly tears, for her body, no matter how swiftly
the blood flowed, was only a shell, earthbound. It was
her spirit, her soul, that was winged, the Lucie that
would endure.

But the demands of the body were riotous, the fierce
pleasures of the senses she had fought to deny herself
but was now powerless to forgo.

'Lucie?' He was lifting her and she buried her face
against his shoulder, her violet eyes closed, her slender
arms clinging around his neck.

'You're so beautiful. You threw a net around me
long ago.'

A *net*. Symbol of captivity when his spirit craved
absolute freedom. How could she tell him she loved
him when he had no use for a woman's heart?

When he lay her down upon his bed, the lamp light
spilled across her white skin, the black silk of her coiled

hair and the swirling violet of her ruffled skirt.

'Look at me, Lucie.' He brought his hands down authoritatively upon her bare shoulders, turning her curved-away body so he could see her more clearly.

She could not open her eyes, voiceless, long drowned.

'You know I mean to have you?'

It was the pattern of her life.

When Julian removed her dress from her with exquisite care, the light beat down upon her pearly skin. He imprisoned her face, the pressure of his fingers on her temples making her open her eyes. 'Are you going to lie there and pretend to suffer me, or are you going to let me love you as I like?'

'But I *long* for you!' she whispered, beyond disguise.

'And I for you.' His beautiful hands found the smooth shape of her breasts. 'I hear music when I'm with you.'

So—an inspiration for ideas, yet such men were rare. The caressing hands were perfect, transfixing her body so they could travel where they liked.

'Lucie, don't weep.' His voice was so tender he might have been talking to a small child.

'It's impossible,' she whispered brokenly.

'What is?'

I'll never hold you, she thought. *Never*.

'Tell me.' He lay down beside her and gathered her right into his arms. 'Tell me, baby. You frighten me.'

'I can't.'

'You feel you lost your dream. What you were born for?'

'What *was* I born for?' she challenged him, illogically in the face of his gentleness driving one small fist into his hard chest. 'For *you*?'

'God, yes!'

The heart beneath her hand pounded and his temper rose to match her own. 'You want this.' He lifted her higher, and covered her mouth with his own. 'You want it . . . want it.'

Lucie became aware that her sensuality was turning her body to flame, differing from the body she had always known. Yet now he had had his victory, the moment's savagery gave way to an unbelievably sensuous slowness where pleasure and pain were the same.

'*Please*, Julian!' Her body was straining for him, arching upwards.

'You are so wonderful to make love to.'

'I can't stand it!' And the intense agitation was there in her eyes.

But his control seemed limitless, the power it had over her. 'You love me, don't you?' The hands that touched her were tender, but his voice was harsh.

'Yes.'

'Yet you know I don't believe in love?'

'Or mercy.'

This had the effect she wanted. As though galvanised Julian took her in a great flare of passion; a drowning, blinding, pulverising rapture, and afterwards when he lay with his head against Lucie's breast, it was she who had the moment's ascendancy.

CHAPTER EIGHT

SHE didn't have to tell Jessie. Jessie knew.

'And has it changed anything?' Jessie gave Lucie one of her penetrating looks.

'No.' Best to face the realisation that this was the case. 'But I'll never find so perfect a lover again.'

'At least until he simply admits he loves you.'

'But he doesn't, Jessie.' Lucie tried to subdue the helpless feelings that swamped her. 'He told me the truth. I'm just part of a fantasy, maybe even a memory.'

'I don't believe it!' Jessie's voice rose in a kind of anger. 'He's maddening, I'll admit, but in spite of it he's been there when you really needed him, and that's the truth.'

'So what shall I do about Joel?' Lucie paused in the act of brushing her hair and gave Jessie a beseeching look.

'You'll have to tell him you can't see him any more.'

Despite his humiliation at Julian's hands, Joel was very hard to convince. 'You're being hysterical about this, Lucie,' he charged her. 'If I were you I'd speak to this psychiatrist of yours about it. You've built Strasberg up in your own mind until he's some kind of an avenging god.'

'I can't see you any more, Joel,' she told him, to put him out of his suffering.

'Oh, I fully intend to see you,' he said grimly, and

even over the telephone Lucie caught the hard flash of his eyes. 'You can't use me, Lucie, and then cast me away. I won't let you.'

'I have to go now, Joel,' Lucie answered quietly. 'Please believe me, I'm sorry about everything, but I simply can't see you any more. It's the only thing I *can* do, release you.'

To her consternation he was waiting for her when she left Van Raven's photographic studio. 'Lucie!' He caught hold of her arm, staring at her accusingly.

'Oh, Joel, *must* you?'

'Yes, I must. What would you like me to do, disappear? My family are expecting an engagement.'

'Your mother, mainly.' Avril Tennant could scarcely comprehend not getting what she wanted. Like Joel.

'Dad too.' Joel tightened his grip on her until she flinched. 'What explanation are you going to give him? I know you like him more than the rest of us put together.'

'I respect him,' Lucie asserted, and tried to pull away.

'Darling!' At once there was pleading in Joel's tone. 'Don't let Strasberg do any more damage. He can't rule your life.'

'I'm making my own life, thank you,' Lucie said.

'So what happened last night?'

'Nothing.' Mercifully Lucie paled rather than coloured. 'Would you excuse me now, Joel? I have another appointment.'

'I'll take you,' his eyes narrowed, 'where to?'

'Sarah's office.'

'No classes with dear Julian?'

'No.' She shielded her violet eyes behind her thick

lashes. 'The hardest thing in life, Joel, is to accept things.'

'There's just too much accepting going around,' Joel told her. 'I'm going to be like Strasberg and seize what I want.'

His attitude bothered Lucie not a little, and she found herself confiding in Sarah.

'But can't he take it like a man?' Sarah pushed back in her swivel chair, the sun on her glorious hair.

'To do that he'd have to be made of sterner stuff.'

'Then why did you encourage him, love?'

'It was the last thing I was trying to do,' Lucie explained wryly. 'At first I thought I was helping him.'

'As I recall, Jessie told me you didn't see him the whole time you were in hospital.'

'I felt he had some kind of a breakdown.' Lucie picked up a glass paperweight and balanced it abstractedly in her hand. 'I've known Joel for a long time, since our student days. Once we were good friends, then everything seemed to change.'

'You mean he fell in love with you.'

'Love can be the devil.'

'Can't it now!' Sarah sighed deeply, absolutely certain of it. 'It sounds like you have a problem.'

'Problems,' Lucie corrected.

'Not with modelling.' Sarah snapped forward and found a sheet of paper on her desk, nodding over it. '*Vogue* want you for their Christmas special edition—smashing gear, and they're talking about a whole new hair-style.'

'But, Sarah. . . .'

'Yes, dear?' Sarah looked up quickly at the odd note in the girl's voice.

'Nothing.' Lucie shrugged. 'I was going to say dancers always wear their hair long.'

'And you haven't give up hope?'

'At least when I'm fully conscious. When I'm asleep I dream I'm dancing: Odette, Odile, Aurora, Swanilda and Giselle. Lately it's been Ley-Ah. . . .'

'That beautiful part, Black Iris?'

'Julian is putting it on again,' Lucie explained.

'Great, I can't wait to see it. He's the most *fantastic* man!'

'Certainly a great choreographer.' Lucie kept her expression smooth. 'Will you tell me what happened when he came to see you?'

Sarah's gaze slid away, out of the window. 'He told me you had it in you to be a great dancer.'

'Oh, well——' Lucie gave a broken laugh.

'He said I had no right to divert you from a great career.'

'He would.' Now Lucie's tender mouth curved into a faint smile. Julian was good at telling people.

'It's all right, I like him,' Sarah said. 'Of course he's so damned attractive he could get away with anything, even murder. When he eventually settled down I found myself promising I would fit my requirements to your splendid talent. You'll have to admit I did my best to keep to your timetable?'

'Yes, Sarah, you did.'

'But you told me yourself, dear child, you had no illusions left at all. You don't find yourself strong enough for a dancer's life.'

'No.' Lucie bent her head.

'You don't sound happy?' Sarah leaned forward, concerned.

'Well, you know what it's like. Jessie told me her champion runner told her he'd never get over being finished with gold medals. Not until the day he died.'

'I guess it's a problem with champions,' Sarah said. 'I regret I never saw you dance, Lucie. Are you sure you're really finished?'

Lucie didn't even flinch. 'I've picked myself up for the last time.'

'Hey, petty, a *smile*!'

'I can't smile,' sighed Lucie.

'Yes, you can, for the cameras.' Sarah grabbed for Lucie's hand and held it. 'Whatever happens in life, Lucie, we have to be sure we do the very best we can.'

When Julian rang her his voice was subtly shadowed with some overtone. 'Are you coming to see Camilla dance Ley-Ah?'

'I don't think I care to.'

'You care.'

For a full moment there was silence, just a humming of the wires.

'Julian, my torment,' sighed Lucie.

'She's no good.'

'What does it matter?'

'It matters a lot.'

'The audience won't know—most of them anyway. Camilla is outstandingly good. If she doesn't identify with Ley-Ah to your satisfaction, you've had no difficulty giving her the role.'

'You're no better,' Julian retorted. 'You had no difficulty dropping it.'

She hung up on him then. Julian, at his most vitriolic.

Doctor Herrington didn't agree.

'You stopped dancing because you were afraid of it?'

'I had the wisdom to see I couldn't. Or rather I would at some time break down. Can you imagine, Doctor, the jeering would be deafening!'

'No.' He shook his shaggy grey head. 'There was a fantastic occasion in my youth when I heard a great soprano break down on the high note of one of her most famous arias. The audience applauded her. She merely held out her hand as if to say, It won't always come, and went on.'

'I should be devastated,' confessed Lucie.

'But then you're very young.'

'So what would you advise me to do?' Lucie forced herself to ask him.

'Go to the ballet. Sit there. Observe. It will take courage, but it seems to me you're a girl of particular character.'

Lucie looked up amazed, but the doctor's expression was quite sincere.

'My God, if I only could!' she sighed.

'You will never be at peace until you're totally satisfied you were right to abandon your career. You could have a few years, a few glorious years. Enough memories to last you the rest of your life.'

'You sound like Julian,' she said.

'I think you love him.'

'Why not? After all, I am a woman.'

Her time was up, and she got up out of her chair, despairing. What was she made of to sit there and watch Camilla dance? Any role but that one and it mightn't have been so difficult. Julian had created *Black Iris* for her. He had no right to give it to Camilla, unless it was to make her suffer. He was a sadist, and she would remember how it was with him till the end of her days.

In the end, Lucie slipped into her very good centre seat about two minutes before the curtain was due to go up on Act One of *Black Iris*. The theatre was packed, yet there was an empty seat beside her. A loner, like herself. In addition, they were late.

She glanced neither to left nor to right, though many people were staring at her, lowering their programmes, trying to place her face.

'I rather think that's Lucienne Gerard,' one beautifully dressed woman with upswept hair whispered to her husband. 'You know, the little dancer who was injured.'

'It says here that the role was created for her.'

'They say she can't dance again, which may not be true.'

Lucie heard them grimly, but over the months she had developed a protective skin. So people were curious? It was understandable. What was not so commendable was their whispering within earshot.

The house lights dimmed and still without turning her head, Lucie turned her knees so a tall man could slip into the seat beside her. A spotlight picked out the conductor of the orchestra, tracked him to his podium in the pit, and the clapping broke out. It was a dazzling ballet, possibly an all-time classic, and the audience were frankly interested in what Camilla Price could do with it. Many of them had witnessed its unforgettable premiere.

The very instant before they made bodily contact,

Lucie knew it was Julian. Then there was the scent of him, and it overtook her in a frenzy.

'*Sit still!*' He brought his hand down firmly on her own, while she sat bolt upright, unsure of what she intended.

The prelude had begun, wonderful music, reminiscent of Verdi, but entirely new, a gateway to dynastic Egypt and the first scene set in the courtyard of the palace.

The curtain went up and there was a mighty muffled gasp as the brilliant spectacle of dancers and the magnificent backdrop unfurled before a thousand eyes.

I can't see this through, Lucie thought. Yet pride held her there like a protective shield. Pride and Julian's iron hand. He wasn't back there with his company, he was out here with her to record her deepest thoughts and feelings. Anger stood her in good stead. It drove the trembling from her body. When the spot came on in readiness for Ley-Ah's entrance, Lucie too put her hands together to applaud. Her throat tightened unbearably, but she would never cry. Camilla looked wonderfully exotic and the set had already had a tremendous impact on the audience. Who was going to notice that she lacked the soft, melting quality Julian had intended? 'Strong' was the word Lucie always thought of to describe Camilla's dancing. Her footwork was brilliant and she had many enthusiastic admirers.

Lucie's hands fell back into her lap, very pale and slender against the glowing scarlet satin of her dress. But they were not permitted to rest there long. Julian took the hand nearest him and thrust his long, elegant fingers through hers, a purposeful gesture Lucie at first saw as a kind of conquering, but which in reality stopped her conditioned agonising and any further disintegration.

In under twenty minutes, her eyes had become his. This was the dance that she loved, and if her own dancing days were over, she was lucky she was still alive. What had Doctor Herrington said? Life was a celebration and the good Lord had shown her how to manage.

Once she leaned her gleaming head towards Julian, speaking in the merest undertone. 'The little one in the corps. . . .'

'Lisa.'

Lisa, of course. She hadn't recognised her in that black wig.

'She's good.'

'Um.'

For all she was matching in with the rest of the corps de ballet, little Lisa, with a lovely singing line, was standing out. Now, with the best part of her mind, Lucie was weighing the performance as a professional. There were no flaws in Camilla's performance. As an ex-principal dancer of the Company she didn't even want to see them. It was just that she didn't jell with Julian's vision. Both of them saw that with clarity.

By the end of Act One, Lucie had lost all sense of self-pity. She was even, though she wasn't yet prepared to admit it, enjoying herself. *Black Iris* unquestionably was a most spectacular and exciting ballet and Julian had created it. The part wasn't irrevocably hers. The ballet would live, but ballerinas only had a short golden age.

Now, with the lights up, they were recognised, as though the one gave the clue to the other's identity.

'That's *him*!' a girl hissed on a raucous note, and nudged her boy-friend. She loved those tall, dark foreign-looking guys with flashing black eyes and high cheekbones. 'You know, *Strasberg*!'

'You've been recognised, Julian,' Lucie said quietly. 'All the time.'

Lucie smiled. She could see that he couldn't care less. Some people were born to move through life turning heads. There were dozens now sitting forward, craneing heads, looking surprised and pleased. It was terrific if a man of vision was also as handsome as a movie star.

'Let's see the rest of this from backstage,' said Julian. 'I don't really care to be out front.'

He took her agreement for granted, holding her hand tightly while they brushed past knees. That was Julian. He didn't ask, you just obeyed.

'Where the devil have you been?' Camilla demanded of Julian as soon as she saw him. 'You saw what that fool Damien did when I went on points. I could murder him!'

'Sorry,' said Damien, and flushed.

'Ready yourselves,' Julian snapped at both of them, his eyes icy.

But now Camilla had seen Lucie and for a moment her triangular face looked like a spitting cat's. 'What's with you, a persecution complex?'

'In what way?' Lucie lifted her delicate black brows.

'You won't be doing this again, will you?' Camilla's face was a mixture of triumph and satisfaction.

'Oh, I don't know.' Lucie said it casually, just to shut her up.

'Well, I do!' Camilla snapped her small white teeth

together, but her hostile face had lost its certainty.
'You've seen the danger. You'd be a fool to try.'

The curtain went up. Applause and Camilla kicked
off.

'Here, Lucie.' One of the boys brought her a high
chair so she could watch from the wings. 'You're looking sensational!'

'Quiet!' Julian snapped. It was obviously beginning
to get to him, the artistic flaw in Camilla's performance. He had to stand there while Camilla acted the
dazzling seductress. She wasn't even supposed to do
that double turn, but she couldn't resist showing off.

Heavens, she was a formidable woman, Lucie
thought. Rarely if ever pleasant, at least to her fellow
dancers. But she and Julian had had an affair. He had
been interested in her for a while.

'. . . Imbecile!'

Julian wasn't caring much for Damien's dancing, but
then wasn't he noticing how Camilla was upstaging
him? Of course he was. Julian noticed everything.
Afterwards there were bound to be heated words.

Act Two over, Camilla pulled Julian's face down and
kissed him. 'How was I?' she asked, her tawny eyes
blazing.

'Perfect beyond description,' said Julian in a voice
that brought forth a general gasp.

'Stinker! So I'm not doing it right?'

'To be truthful, no.'

'Okay, so get somebody else!' Camilla's eyes flashed.

Damien's brown eyes doubled in size. 'God, you
wouldn't do anything horrible like that, would you?'

'Why not?'

'Go and get Sally,' Julian told him.

'Sally? Now wait a minute,' Camilla saw her mistake. 'Isn't this *fabulous*! Are you throwing me out, Julian?'

'Didn't you say you were leaving?'

He does it perfectly, Lucie thought. Of course he's crushed me in the past, and now from triumph, Camilla was looking drooping and wretched.

'You know I wasn't serious. I could never be serious. I could never leave *you*.'

'How extremely improbable,' Julian drawled, looking bored.

'Please, darling, I'm so sorry.'

'I only wish you would dance Ley-Ah instead of acting like a wanton.'

Lucie wished fervently that she might pick up her feet and run away, but they were all trapped by the conversation.

'If you must be bloody spiteful,' Camilla snapped.

'Did you hear that?' Damien hissed in Lucie's ear. 'From that bitch, Camilla!'

Then all further communication was over. The orchestra started up, gaining power, and Julian said curtly, 'Get on.'

Afterwards, though the audience appeared to have thoroughly enjoyed themselves if one counted the curtain calls, there were many destructive words said. Camilla went on endlessly, always coming back to the same thing. Julian was a fiend.

'Gosh, I loathe women,' Damien told Lucie. 'Though I always fancied you. You're a wise girl, getting out of this company. Come to think of it, it's been terrible since you left. Julian was never as slashing as this. I mean, he used to give you hell, but you have to think he loved to see you dance.'

'Ah, little Lucie!' Camilla came up to them, still in her stage make-up. 'So beautiful! Poor unlucky little Lucie, had a dreadful accident.'

'You'll be having one yourself in the not too distant future,' Damien said gamely. 'Leave Lucie alone.'

'But how is it, darling,' Camilla opened wide her heavily made-up eyes, 'you inspire this protective feeling? Is it because you're such a frail little thing or because you've led such a blameless life?'

'Where on earth did you get *that* idea?' Lucie drawled with masterly sophistication, and even Damien glanced at her sideways.

'You sort of do look different at that.'

But Camilla wasn't being humorous. A look of fear crossed her face that instantly vanished. 'When are you going to marry your boy-friend?' she asked.

'Oh, I think marriage spoils things,' Damien said quickly. 'I mean, it's so hideously restricting.'

'Shut up,' Camilla said with charming rudeness. 'What exactly *is* it you're doing here anyway?' she asked Lucie sharply. 'I mean, it's so stupid to torture yourself.'

'You never know,' Lucie said sweetly, 'I might be coming back again.'

'Over my dead body!' Camilla shook her head violently. 'Take my advice, marry your rich boy-friend.'

She swept past them and Damien drew an exaggerated sigh of relief. 'I don't know whether to hate that woman or feel sorry for her. Can it be true that she and Julian once loved each other?'

'Or some such situation.'

'You don't think Julian could love anyone?' Damien asked.

'What about you?'

'He's a man of strong feelings,' Damien said thoughtfully. 'Very strong feelings indeed. I suppose in a sense he builds a cage around himself. I suppose most creative artists do. He simply has to have the time and the quiet to create miracles like *Black Iris*. Of course, what got into him tonight was the memory of you. You were absolutely perfect. I got high just partnering you. You have some power that makes your partner match you. It's always like a contest with Camilla. She's a show pony first and an artist second.'

Whatever she was, she could dance, Lucie thought. And I can't. Too damn bad.

Along the passageway a boy was wandering around with a huge basket of flowers, and Lucie went forward to help him, though she knew they were for Camilla.

'Miss Price?' He pushed the basket of flowers at her as though he hardly cared.

'I'm afraid she's already left the theatre.'

'Then where am I supposed to leave 'em?'

'I'll take care of them,' Lucie offered. It was a magnificent bouquet and it must have cost a fortune; roses, carnations, gladioli like pink swords. The note was attached to the basket with more pink ribbon. Without choosing to, it was easy to read what was written in a heavy black hand.

> To my beauty and joy,
> Ever your
> Julian.

Julian. There had to be at least a hundred dollars' worth of flowers there. The basket alone was a work of art. Well, she had always known of their relationship.

Flowers from Julian. She had received bouquets galore after she had danced *Black Iris*, but nothing from Julian, only a kiss. The briefest, glancing acknowledgment, unequalled by anyone but him, before or since.

It was Camilla who had earned the distinction of flowers. Obviously, for all their antics and intense clashes, they were bound by a million threads. Lucie had known that at the outset. Camilla had a position in his life, a stature she could never have.

Lucie glanced around quickly, her eyes resting on Julian's tall, striking figure as he stood talking to Alistair Thomas, the country's most influential ballet critic. His beautiful, expressive hands were slicing the air and Alistair Thomas was looking up at him in fascination. After all, he had already acknowledged Julian as a genius.

The bouquet released her, though the pain would never heal. The most terrible thing was that he had never lied to her. He had never told her he loved her. Love was *her* disease.

'Well, what are you standing there for?' Damien asked, and looked down at the floral basket with a show of amazement. 'Flowers from Julian for Camilla? Never, never, never. She probably sent them to herself.'

All of a sudden Lucie felt very tired. She put the basket down and gave a little helpless gesture, turning herself in an instant into poignancy incarnate.

'Would you give these to Julian?' she said. 'He probably didn't realise Camilla would leave so hurriedly.'

'Sure.' Damien plucked the basket off the floor. 'Sweetie, you look ready to cry.'

'No.' Lucie shook her glossy head. 'I'm just a little tired.'

'If you give me a moment I'll run you home,' Damien offered.

'Thanks, Damien, but I have the car.'

'Right then. Be careful, love.'

Lucie drove most of the way home in a daze and ran up the path to the open doorway where Jessie was waiting.

'What's this, you can't wait to tell me?' In truth Jessie had been very anxious, but Lucie had insisted on going alone. Then too, as Jessie had omitted to mention, Julian had called to ascertain the number of Lucie's ticket.

Lucie didn't answer until she was right through the door. 'A full house,' she said with forced composure. 'Camilla was brilliant without taking on the essence of the role.'

'And you?' Jessie was looking at her searchingly, 'how do *you* feel?'

'Released, Jessie,' Lucie said quietly.

'Well then,' Jessie was aware of her upset, 'I've made supper.'

Lucie managed to smile. 'I'll just slip out of my dress. Won't be long.'

She was half-way through to her room when the phone range.

'Now who could that be at this time of night?' Jessie demanded from the hallway.

Don't let it be Julian, Lucie prayed.

It was Julian. Lucie took several small jerky steps towards the phone, but Jessie answered it for her.

'I'll get it. Why, hello, Julian.' Jessie looked up at Lucie's face for a long moment, mixed feelings chasing across her broad, reliable face. 'Well, she is here, an' all. A few moments ago. . . . Quite all right. . . . Didn't she? How odd. Oh, I don't know, Julian. If you *must*.'

'Is he coming here?' Lucie steadied herself against a chair.

'What did you say, Julian. I didn't hear that.'

'Tell him I never want to see him again.' Lucie's legs were shaking so much she had to sit down.

'Tell him yourself, love.' Jessie held out the phone.

She couldn't sit there sickly like a coward, so she got up and took the receiver from Jessie, who patted her hand comfortingly.

'Hello, Julian.'

His voice was at its most cutting. 'Is there any chance at all that you're going to grow up?'

'I'll certainly try.'

'Thomas wanted to speak to you.'

'Really? An ex-ballerina?'

'Oh, never mind, then,' he said violently. 'You're determined to write yourself off and you're going to be damned unhappy while you're doing it.'

'Do you want to say any more?' Lucie asked politely.

'You're a fool.'

'Goodbye, Julian,' she said, after she had hung up. 'He was there tonight beside me,' she told Jessie, her violet eyes suddenly welling with tears. 'For the first time in a long time I felt almost normal, not damaged. I actually forgot myself.'

'Then what happened?' Jessie asked sadly.

'Just a little thing. Julian sent Camilla flowers—a huge basket. It was the words more than anything.'

She repeated them in an impassive voice, but Jessie heard them frowning.

'One can be so wrong, Lucie. Did you actually recognise Julian's writing?'

'Yes, it was Julian's. Bold and black.'

'It doesn't sound like him,' Jessie said dubiously, 'considering all the agonising he does over you.'

'Julian, agonising?' Lucie asked with a twisted smile. 'The most he has ever felt for me was desire.'

Jessie clicked her tongue and shook her head but said nothing at all. What did she know of men, after all? They were absolute enigmas.

A few days later, Joel's father invited her to lunch, and because it was obviously his intention to find out, Lucie explained the situation between Joel and herself.

'I thought as much.' The pleasant expression on Grant Tennant's face dissolved into one of deepest regret. 'In any case, it wouldn't work out. Joel has nothing to offer you—anyway, at this stage. His mother has always given him so much attention the boy is spoiled rotten and utterly querulous when he doesn't get his own way.'

'Your own son!' Lucie exclaimed sadly.

'You know it's true, my dear. This will be the first time in his life Joel has ever been denied all he's wanted. And anyway, it's my fault. I should have been much firmer with Avril, but Joel was always her little boy, finer, more sensitive than either Gavin or myself. What he really needed was toughening up.'

'But isn't he working well now?' Lucie asked quietly.

Grant Tennant bit back an acerbic comment and merely said: 'No.'

'I'm sorry. Sorry for you. Sorry for Joel.'

'I can see that, my dear, in your shining eyes. Unfortunately he'll take it hard. So too will Avril. Apart from one other, you're the only girl she's ever deemed suitable for her son.'

'And the other?'

'May well win him.' Grant Tennant put his wine glass down abruptly. 'You've told Joel, have you?'

'I have.' Lucie looked directly into the fine dark eyes. 'I hope he'll forgive me.'

'What for? For being so beautiful?' Grant Tennant said gallantly. 'You were very good to try and help him when you did. After that—well, I'm afraid we all put the pressure on you. Leave it to me, my dear. I'll make the position quite clear to Joel. I know he can become difficult when he's thwarted.'

Unpleasant as it was, Lucie knew it was necessary for Grant Tennant to speak to his son. Joel was not given to going away quietly.

One more painful phone call where Joel started off very sweetly and finished off abusively, and Lucie heard no more. Later she learned from a mutual friend that Joel had been transferred to the Perth office of one of his father's companies, and her trembling heart remembered the words he had called her. Even now she recoiled from them to the extent that it was difficult to recall the good times she and Joel had shared together. Once they had both been so young and innocent, two other people. It was appalling how passions changed lives.

CHAPTER NINE

WEEKS went by when Lucie had more modelling and photographic work than she could handle. It seemed she did nothing but get up early, dash around town all day mostly without lunch, stagger home late, then fall into bed so she would be fit enough to do the whole thing again the next day. Being beautiful was a bore, and too time-consuming. Some of the other girls were narcissistic to the point of adoring themselves, while others were frankly neurotic about diets. It took little or nothing to emaciate Lucie, and Jessie, regarding her almost breakable figure, was moved to protest.

'Turn sideways, love, and I can't see you!'

'Perhaps I'd better start having milk shakes,' suggested Lucie.

'You'd better stop all this rushing around. The pace isn't good for you—even a young girl.'

The next week Lucie accepted an assignment in Tahiti and as Sarah went along on the trip, for a few days Lucie found time to relax. It was a glowing part of the world, bathed in an incredible light, and Lucie could well see how Gauguin had found such powerful inspiration.

For the first time in her life she allowed her camellia white skin to turn palest gold. Dancers shunned suntans, but now it no longer mattered. She thanked God her demons left her alone save in sleep. She did not want to think of her old life, though this new one was not of her choosing. Had she *had* any choice?

It was Sarah who read the article in the paper, clicking her tongue in distress.

'Why, look here——' she caught Lucie's hand to gain her attention, 'Julian's mother's died!'

'My—my God!'

Sarah nodded and turned the paper around. 'Sophia Strasberg, one of the most illustrious ballerinas the world has ever known. . . .'

Fragile Lucie seemed to shrink in her chair. 'She couldn't have been very old.'

'Not old,' Sarah confirmed, her voice saddened. 'Fifty-three.'

'Does it mention Julian?' Lucie couldn't bear to read the article at all.

'Of course, quite a bit. He's in New York.'

'Poor Julian!' Lucie whispered.

'There's a lot more about the father—brilliant architect. Do you want me to read it?'

'No.' Once Julian, so virile, so powerful, had been a lonely little boy. Probably at that time he had wanted an ordinary mother, one who would always be there with loving words and open arms. Was worship an adequate substitute for close communication?

'Well, I'm sorry to hear that,' Sarah said. 'I really am. No wonder Julian is the phenomenon he is, with such a background. I suppose once he's home again his own world will call him. Few people as brilliant as Julian can resist the finest setting.'

'I suppose not,' Lucie agreed quietly. 'The company would fall apart without him. No one has his command.'

'Ah well, we can't sit around feeling miserable,' Sarah pushed up from the round table with its gaily patterned beach umbrella overhead. 'Van's got some sightseeing adventure lined up.' She threw back her head like a sunflower. 'My, isn't this sun glorious! You know you look fabulous with that tan—painting the lily, as it were. What do you think about Van's idea with that scuba gear?'

Lucie wanted to cry, but couldn't. Time later when there was no one around to witness her emotion.

But Julian did return and one of the women's magazines ran a splendidly put together feature about the life and career of a his beautiful mother. It overtook Lucie to the extent that she went back to her old teacher Patricia Lowe, ex-principal dancer with the Royal Ballet, who had returned to her own country to teach after retirement.

'To do what, Lucie?' Patricia asked.

'God knows.' Lucie tried to explain herself. 'It was that article about Sophia Strasberg that decided me. In her youth she had tremendous setbacks.'

'She was magic,' Patricia said. 'A great star that only appears once in every hundred years. No one knows precisely what goes into making such magic. She was a wonderful technician, but there are others. She was beautiful, but plain girls providing they've got good eyes, can be beautiful made up. I saw her numerous times and in every role she was superb. The musicality, the acting! In as much as any of us can be perfect she was perfect. Have you seen Julian, by the way?'

'No, not for some time.'

'More fool you,' Patricia said not unkindly. 'I saw him as soon as he got back.'

'Is he all right?'

'You know Julian,' Patricia moved her hand to her nape to smoothe her impeccable chignon. 'His deepest feelings he keeps very much to himself. I suppose he learned it in childhood, and lessons hard learned are never forgotten. Sophia was a goddess, but she was never cut out to be a mother. Julian was never denied anything material but it was rare for him to have his mother's company. His father's too, I'm sure. Both brilliant people leading intensely dedicated lives. I'm sure Julian must have suffered.'

'He must have been upset?' Lucie asked vaguely.

'All he said was, *it's over*. He spoke about you.'

Lucie walked over to the barre and put her hand on it. 'What did he say?'

'That you were a little fool. He was in fine lacerating form. He's convinced you have it in you to make a great dancer, and your trouble is more or less psychological and so on.'

'That's what I've come back to find out.'

'Then find out we shall,' Patricia promised. 'Whether your body can stand the strain remains to be seen, but we shall work on the assumption it can. You are an ex-dancer who's taken time off and must now get back to the disciplines of class. I don't anticipate any absences, Lucie. If you are serious, you'll have to rearrange your life.'

Lucie nodded, her small oval face intensely dedicated and unafraid. 'I promise you, from tomorrow.'

Patricia responded immediately, drawing herself up in the old attitude of authority. 'You were always my favourite anyway. I'm sure you're doing the right thing. Since Julian agrees with me I feel encouraged to start. I shall expect you here, come what may, at ten-thirty each morning. Afternoon classes will begin at two.'

It was the evening of the same day, and Lucie sat on Julian's front steps waiting for him to come home. It was almost dark and there was no sign of him. Probably he wouldn't come home at all. She had been waiting, half hidden by flowering bushes, for the best part of an hour, wondering why she had come. Love, loneliness, a sincere desire to offer sympathy. Most likely he wanted nothing from her at all, no overture of any kind. Certainly not her love. She even had to consider he might be hostile. That was if he ever came.

Ten minutes later she heard the unmistakable sound of the Porsche's engine and as she looked arund cautiously it swung up the drive and instead of heading for the garage made the semi-circle to the base of the stairs.

Now that he was here, she was like a wild creature, staring this way and that for a possible line of flight.

'*Lucie!*' The brilliant black eyes flashed up to her small figure.

She rose from her childlike position, standing at the top of the short, broad flight of steps. 'I had to see you, Julian,' she said, staring at him with emotion-darkened eyes.

'Now suddenly you have to see me—what's so urgent?' He slammed the car door and came towards her with the purposeful tread of a panther.

All my love for you, she thought, but dared not mention.

'Such a sad little face!' Now he was beside her, looking down at her.

'I'm sorry, Julian, about your mother.'

'Thank you.' He said it so grimly he looked almost sinister.

'Do you want me to go away?' She half turned, helpless as always in his presence.

'In a little while, perhaps,' he said coolly. 'You must forgive me, Lucie, I'm just so amazed to see you here.'

'You've always mattered, Julian.'

'But I'm too wicked for a beautiful innocent like you.'

Lucie said nothing, and after a moment he opened the front door and stood back to allow her to go in.

'I've seen your face a thousand times,' he murmured, his black eyes resting on her downbent head, the flushed cheeks. 'Airports, newspaper stands—it's difficult to shut you out.'

'I don't think I can handle my new career,' she told him.

'It seems like fate, doesn't it? Your not being able to handle anything.'

'Julian——' She turned breathlessly, not realising he was so near her.

'What is it now?' He looked unbearably arrogant.

'Everything I want to say to you comes out the wrong way.'

'Possibly this is the reason we don't get on.'

'I went to see Patricia,' she told him.

'Really?' This very politely. 'You prefer her to me?'

'It was reading about your mother.'

Julian shrugged his shoulders. 'The path to greatness, Lucie, is very steep. I don't think you've got it in you.'

'Certainly never like your mother.'

'You know absolutely nothing about her.'

'No.' It had been a waste of time coming. Julian could only make a woman suffer. Lucie lowered her head and linked her trembling fingers. 'You're very intolerant of me, aren't you, Julian?'

'More nearly at the end of my tether.' His vibrant voice was full of self-mockery. 'Are you going to sit down?'

'I don't think I should stay.'

'You seem obsessed by the thought that something might happen to you,' he commented.

'Not any more, you look too angry, unreachable.'

'A pose I can't break, Lucie.' He said it in an odd, ironic voice. 'You're a compassionate little thing, I can see that. You've come here to offer sympathy?'

'Yes.'

'Think of that! You lock yourself away for weeks, and now you're going to extend mercy.'

His defences were like a physical barrier. He was all pride and male arrogance, and he would forever turn the tables on her.

'Now when it no longer matters, I can tell you I loved you,' she said quietly. 'But you won't allow yourself to be loved. I accept that.'

'So I'm to lose you?' he asked with appalling mockery.

'How can you lose what you never had?'

'Oh, I had you,' he returned harshly, flickering lights in his dark eyes. 'I'll hear your little cry all the nights of my life.'

'And I'm *glad*!' Her beautiful skin was suffused with

colour. 'I'm glad you'll remember how you wounded me.'

Julian muffled an oath and his fingers bit into the spare flesh of her side. 'What are words anyway? This is the only thing that really matters.'

They came together with a yearning so violent it was agonising, discovering in each other a mutual need that was shattering. Julian's grip was powerful and crushing, his mouth consuming the cushioned sweetness of the lips beneath his.

It was delirium, and Lucie knew if she went with it the same would happen as before; Julian's body on hers, his hands, his mouth arousing her so that they shared a pleasure to wonder at; greater than any pleasure she had ever known.

'*Please*, Julian!' She flung herself back so violently he relaxed his hold. Another moment and there was nothing she would not give him.

His voice was driven, beset by emotion. 'I want you so much it's agony.' His hand moved to her breast, palm circling, thumb teasing the aroused nipple. 'I've never known a woman I couldn't live without. It gives me no peace at all.'

'And yet you're angry,' she said wonderingly. 'Think of it. You're *angry* because a mere woman has some dominion over you.'

'I know if you left me I'd be all alone.'

For Julian it was the greatest admission, and her breath caught. 'Then why do you fear what's in your own heart?'

'My heart has never taken part in my love affairs for a very long time.' Julian made a harsh sound of self-derision and released her.

'And Camilla?' she asked quietly.

'Wonderful—we're going to talk about Camilla!' he mocked.

'You called her your beauty and joy.'

He looked at her startled, then laughed. 'Who did she tell that to, her hairdresser?'

Lucie turned away. 'What happened—*happens*—between you and Camilla is nothing to do with me.'

'Don't be stupid,' he said bluntly.

'*Tell* me!' she begged.

'Sorry, darling, I don't give a damn what you think. I've told you before, Camilla is ancient history, but you obviously don't trust me. It's like that with women, I think. No trust. In my world there are women everywhere—beautiful, graceful women. A lot of them go through some little dream cycle when they imagine they're in love with me. So it has to be trust.'

'*I've* never lied to you,' she said, her face as vulnerable as a girl's could ever get.

'Then I don't suppose you've had to. Oh, what the hell!' Frustration blazed in his brilliant eyes. 'The only reality I seem to know is when I have you in my arms. Everything else is all jangling words.' He flung himself into a chair with the arrogant grace Lucie half dreaded, half adored, staring up at her, wary and strangely aroused.

'Listen,' she said lightly, 'why don't you see my psychiatrist?'

'Bitch!'

'Talk to him.' She wanted to go to him, sit in his lap, wind her arms around his neck, instead she held herself aloof, a small girl unaware of her own beauty.

'And then as a matter of course I offer to marry you.

God, wouldn't I have plenty of reason to go off my rocker then!'

'But *why*?'

'Why?' His beautiful voice was jerky. 'My mind's not clear on the answer. You could make me suffer too easily. Women find a man's weaknesses and use them. And a woman you *loved*!' His smouldering dark eyes gazed at her intently. 'You don't even know how beautiful you are, Lucie. I mean beautiful right through. You shine from the very depths of your being. No, don't look amazed, it's true. At the moment you're only a child, but you could be a big star. I remind you, not without *me*, but millions could come to idolise you.'

'So even if this happened, what could it mean?' She was bewildered and showing it.

'You don't think my mother was always faithful to my father, do you? She had many secret romances and others she didn't bother to hide. She was a very beautiful and clever woman, but she wasn't in the least, how shall I put it, kind.'

'Your father was aware of her affairs?'

'Do you think he didn't *mind*? I would have killed her!' His hands moved expressively.

'So what has this to do with you and me?' asked Lucie.

'You'd need to know what would happen if you ever tried to get away from me. Never, never.'

'And you're the one who speaks about trust.' She shook her head, dazed and confused by the tangle of emotions.

'You're just a child.' Julian leaned forward, stretching out his arm so their hands touched.

'No, I'm a woman, don't you see that? You should, Julian.'

He sighed deeply and put her palm against his cheek. 'Go away, little one. I'm afraid of what might happen if you don't.'

'I love you,' she said, her voice shaky with the suppression of tears.

'You won't go back on it ever? How can you tell?'

She could see the cynicism in his eyes, bitter memories from the past. 'You might have said love can last. It can, Julian. My mother's tragedy was the love she bore for only one man—my father. She lost him when I was only three. If you think I have looks I got them from my mother. There must have been other men who admired her, but none she found to compare with my father. Fidelity even to a memory is not extinct.'

'And loving a woman no greater tyranny.'

There was nothing she could possibly say that would be persuasive. Julian had to come to it himself.

So Lucie worked, determined she would not be defeated by the fear of failure, but many times she caught Patricia's expression and read correctly the unspoken thought: Will her legs hold out?

They did—absolutely. So Patricia cried out with rare praise: 'What I wouldn't give for a twenty-two-year-old body! The speed—where do you get it from?'

Feeling wonderfully lighthearted, Lucie whipped into a double turn, then another. If she had to she could do the thirty-two fouettés as in *Swan Lake*. Her courage, the wonderful, saving courage that all dancers needed, had come back. It was courage and confidence that made the difference. Fear could cripple, it could even set the stage for an injury.

It wasn't until she had stopped that Lucie realised Patricia and her flock of dancers were standing still. They had been standing there watching her, admiring, learning.

'I'm *never* going to be a dancer,' one little girl with her hair all done up in plaits told a friend. 'Did you just see her balances? They're splendid. I thought she was supposed to have a weak leg? They're extremely strong.'

Undemonstrative, Patricia hugged her. 'Good girl, Lucie! I'm pleased with you.'

'*Merci.*'

'Wait!' Patricia called out to the flying figure. 'Lucie, I have to speak to you.'

'Yes?' Lucie turned. 'Two minutes, Pat, and I have to run—a booking.'

'Julian has worked out a new pas de deux. He wants you to go over.'

'When?' Excitement swelled in her and the perennial sense of hopelessness.

'As soon as you can.' Patricia surveyed her calmly. 'He's up to date on your progress.'

'You'd tell him anything, wouldn't you?'

'Just about.' Patricia's lovely smile made her thin face look quite youthful. 'If I were twenty years younger I'd fall madly in love with him, the heathen!'

The photographic session took well over an hour and afterwards, rather fearfully, Lucie went to the phone. Julian would be in the middle of a class, but there would be somebody there to answer the phone.

'Darling!' It was Damien, and he recognised her voice instantly.

'Julian wants me to come over,' she went on. 'Does that mean now?'

'Hold it, sweetie, and I'll ask him.'

Lucie waited, tapping her foot. A new pas de deux—that meant something that was technically frightfully demanding. Ah well!

Damien again, swearing and apologising. 'Sorry, love, just tripped over Anne's stupid bag. You'd make a great mistake not coming at once. Take a cab, and a tranquilliser for Julian might help. He's in a filthy state of mind.'

He was, at the best of times, Lucie thought, but when he wasn't, one forgot all the other times.

'Go home,' he told all the others when Lucie arrived. 'Except you, Damien, of course.'

But now the others wanted to stay, interested in what was happening.

'Tomorrow,' Julian said. 'Ten-thirty.' And his tone left them no reason to stay.

'Come here, Lucie.'

She went to him and he took her hand. 'I want this pas de deux performed in under a month and I want you and Damien to dance it for me. Warm up at the barre and when you're ready I'll take you both through the steps. The lifts I'll demonstrate first. They're spectacular, but you're a feather and Damien knows how to show his ballerina off.'

Damien, handsome, muscular, brown-eyed and eager, looked pleased. Lucienne was his all-time favourite partner and anything of Julian's had to be very effective.

After fifteen minutes of conventional barre Julian called sharply for them to begin. There was a deep cleft of concentration between his winged black brows the handsome mouth pulled down as though he was about to ask a lot of them.

'Now this is what I require of you. It will be difficult, but you *will* try.'

It went on for an hour, but Lucie and Damien were very fast learners. Besides, they were experiencing an irresistible elation. What Julian had created was something not traditional nor modern, but timeless; a love duet using the most beautiful and exciting techniques. His was an immense dance vocabulary and he had fully exploited the potential of his two dancers.

Damien in his mid-twenties was at the peak of his powers, immensely strong, muscular, when was necessary for the impressive lifts, but wonderfully expressive and supple. Lucienne, the total dancer, with a virtuoso technique that was only there to serve an increasingly poetic lyricism, a lyricism that was given to a very few.

It was all happening so spontaneously Julian had even become gentle. 'We don't want to overdo it, Lucie.'

'No, it's all right,' she would turn to smile at him.

'Now forget you've got bones. I want you to float back until you nearly touch the floor.'

The most spectacular lift when she was held like a bird in flight on Damien's straight up arm presented the only insurmountable difficulty. In mid-air with one leg bent, Lucie had to fully extend her other leg behind her, holding the pose effortlessly, while Damien's arm like iron was not permitted to even quiver.

'Here, let me show you.' Julian started to throw Lucie around like a feather.

'But you're taller than I am, much stronger.'

'It's Lucie who has to help you. She has to so hold her body she takes the weight off your arm.'

They tried it, and Damien's arm wobbled alarmingly.

'Don't drop her.'

'*Hell!*' Damien was jangled by the note of near fear in Julian's voice.

'Forget it for the moment,' said Julian. 'We'll go on.'

The rest was easier, though it hurt, and afterwards Julian dismissed Damien and asked Lucie to remain behind.

'So far, so good,' he told her.

She swallowed, wondering if he was going to go back to that lift.

'How have you been?' he asked, for the first time touching on the personal.

'Busy.'

'Patricia believes you're better than you ever were. I agree.'

'Do you?' She scarcely dared look at him.

'Yes. You're perfect.'

'I'm not doing too well on that lift,' she sighed.

'It's not all that easy to soar like a bird. Damien is strong. He'll get the hang of it, but you have to help him. You have to gather yourself right into your centre. You have to leap like an acrobat. You have to be absolutely fearless.'

'Anything else?' she smiled wryly.

'Come, let me show you.'

'And what is it called?' She gave him her beautiful, jewelled glance. 'Our pas de deux?'

'*Elysium.*'

'Paradise.'

Something in his expression made her draw in her breath.

'Now, Lucie,' he ordered, not taking his eyes off her.

With Damien it was a matter of two beautiful trained bodies in complete accord. In part, Lucie was amazingly gifted. She could simulate love, but as soon as Julian touched her, she melted. Her body was fluid, floating, weightless.

There was no question of forcing. She ran, she leapt with tremendous elevation, shot up into his arms and from there was carried like a rising bird, her left leg bent, her right leg extended way up behind her, both arms winged back, the head lifted.

The whole line was unbelieveably beautiful, streamlined, aerodynamic. They held it and held it, and it was a kind of a glory. Then Julian brought her down slowly, with perfect control, his hands high up beneath her breasts, not supportive now but explicitly sensual.

'I congratulate you, Lucie,' he said.

'Everything is easy with you,' she said blissfully.

'You're very sure.' Unexpectedly the vivid, handsome face was grave.

'Sure of what, Julian?' she asked wonderingly. 'That I love you?'

'Please, I want to know.'

'Why?'

'I *need* to know.' Desperation and curtness were equally mixed.

'I'll always love you, Julian,' she said tenderly. 'I'll never love anyone else.'

'When I'm so cruel to you? When I don't deserve you?'

'Even then.' She closed her eyes and turned her face along his heart. 'Tell me what you want me to do and I'll do it. Tell me what you want me to be and I'll be it.'

'*Lucie.*' That dark, arrogant voice sounded unbearably moved, and his free hand caressed the satiny nape of her neck. 'Let me take care of you for always.'

'You'd like me for a mistress?' Her gentle voice held a trace of laughter.

'Never! You'll never leave me, my wife-to-be.'

'It appears then that you love me.' She lifted her head and her beautiful violet eyes were filled with love and laughter.

'Of course I do.' His voice was cool, but it wasn't matched by the look in his eyes and the strength of his arms. 'I loved you long before I would ever admit it. Now I can see I'll have to admit it all the time.'

'Not really,' Lucie said dreamily, 'just try it once more.'

'I love you,' he said, very low and caressing. 'I love you . . . love you.' He said it over and over until his mouth closed on hers.

Harlequin Plus

THE STORY OF CAMILLE

Camille, an American stage play, was originally a novel and drama (*Dame aux Camélias*) written by Alexandre Dumas in 1848. A touching and sentimental love story, it concerns a beautiful French courtesan named Camille, who leaves the Parisian round of frivolity for Armand Duval—a man who, unlike her other admirers, has only his love to offer.

Armand takes Camille to live in the country, because of her racking cough, and the camellias he grows in his garden replace the ones she always wore in Paris. But their happiness is brief. In Armand's absence Camille is visited by his father, who persuades Camille that her poor reputation will disgrace Armand's family. Putting her lover's honor before her own happiness, Camille returns to Paris without explanation. But her heart is with Armand. And her cough becomes worse.

By the time Armand learns the true motive for Camille's desertion, she is on her deathbed. He arrives to find her wearing the simple flowers he once gave her. As he declares his love, she dies in his arms.

Camille has inspired an opera—*La Traviata*—and a film. *Camille* the film starred the legendary Greta Garbo, and for her role she read everything she could find about Alexandre Dumas's mistress, the real-life woman on whom the character was based. The story of a rehabilitated courtesan, a little dated, a little exaggerated, succeeds perhaps because it was drawn from actual life; but some say it is the symbol of the fragile camellia that captures the imagination of audiences everywhere.

Harlequin Romances

The books that let you escape
into the wonderful world of romance!
Trips to exotic places...interesting
plots...meeting memorable people...
the excitement of love.... These are
integral parts of Harlequin Romances –
the heartwarming novels read by
women everywhere.

Many early issues are now available.
Choose from this great selection!

Choose from this list of Harlequin Romance editions.*

*Some of these book were originally published under different titles.

Relive a great love story...
with Harlequin Romances
Complete and mail this coupon today!

Harlequin Reader Service

In the U.S.A.
1440 South Priest Drive
Tempe, AZ 85281

In Canada
649 Ontario Street
Stratford, Ontario N5A 6W2

Please send me the following Harlequin Romance novels. I am enclosing my check or money order for $1.50 for each novel ordered, plus 75¢ to cover postage and handling.

☐ 982	☐ 1156	☐ 1180	☐ 1195	☐ 1221
☐ 984	☐ 1162	☐ 1181	☐ 1200	☐ 1222
☐ 1015	☐ 1168	☐ 1183	☐ 1203	☐ 1237
☐ 1048	☐ 1172	☐ 1184	☐ 1204	☐ 1238
☐ 1126	☐ 1173	☐ 1186	☐ 1214	☐ 1248
☐ 1151	☐ 1175	☐ 1187	☐ 1215	☐ 1314

Number of novels checked @ $1.50 each = $_____

N.Y. and Ariz. residents add appropriate sales tax. $_____

Postage and handling $____.75

TOTAL $_____

I enclose _____
(Please send check or money order. We cannot be responsible for cash sent through the mail.)

Prices subject to change without notice.

NAME _____
(Please Print)

ADDRESS _____
(APT. NO.)

CITY _____

STATE/PROV. _____

ZIP/POSTAL CODE _____

Offer expires September 30, 1983   30356000000